First Edition

ASIN: B0FC625JYP

ISBN (trade): 979-8-9991778-1-0

Book Cover: Pia

Editing: Brandy Gibson

Social Media Coordinator: Tawny Gratto

Social Media Group Moderator: Ashley Sullivan

PA: Sarah Toon

Marketing & PR: Wildfire Marketing Solutions

UNHOLY VOWS

SARA MCCLAFLIN

Prologue

SELENE

I watch everyone gather around the kitchen table, laughter rising beneath flickering candlelight. The warmth of family drifts through the room.

Ophelia started these family barbecues after she mated with my nephew, Julian—her way of bringing light to a world that was mostly surrounded by darkness and fire. Somehow, her vision worked.

Our family has grown exponentially since Theron and I mated. Between us and his brother, there are seven kids.

Possibly a few grandchildren on the way soon, depending on how certain events go.

Ophelia is laughing with her sister, Arabella, while my son, Seth, leans in—smirking, of course. The room hums with life.

I love hearing the house so full of life. But I know that there is something that I have to tell them. Something that is about to alter our world forever. Something that will break the peace and harmony that we built.

Balance has shifted. Everyone can feel it.

Just the other day, Theron and I were walking with Evander and Liora when we saw the moon flicker. A breeze came next. It was ice cold to the point a shiver shot up our spines.

The four of us, ancient as we are, frozen in terror.

There has only ever been *one* other time I felt that same chill.

1692.

The year I died. The time that everything changed. The story I swore I'd never speak again.

Until now.

"Everyone," I say, trying to get their attention. Evander and Liora know exactly what we're about to talk about. This isn't going to be pretty.

I look at Arabella and Ophelia. I know that they are going to have a hard time with this.

"This is about Cassius."

Arabella's lips press into a thin line. Ophelia's fingers curl slightly around her glass. Their men instinctively step in front of them a fraction, protecting from the name itself.

Thankfully, no one interrupts.

"He tipped the balance," I say. " with the knowledge he possesses."

Julian frowns. "What kind of knowledge?"

"The kind mortals were never supposed to have." I scan the table. "He started telling the Creeds how to make deals—how to offer souls, how to trade one life for another —and now *they're* spreading it. The circle that they are in is spreading it to one another. And now people are making deals—rushing in like it's some kind of virtue."

Owen's voice is quiet. "Martyrs."

"No," I say. "*They think* they're martyrs. I made a deal

like that. I know what it takes. What it breaks. The pain you carry for the rest of your existence."

I have to take a second before I continue. The memories are threatening to rush back in full force.

With a steadying breath, I speak. "But now? People are offering themselves for strangers, for causes, for spectacle. They don't understand the price. They think it's noble. They think they're doing the right thing for someone else." I shake my head. "They're so very wrong."

Seth leans forward. "So, what? We're looking at a generation of self made sacrifices?"

"We're looking at people who've been handed power without understanding consequence," I say. "They're not doing it out of love or desperation. They're doing it to be seen. To be admired. To feel… important. The Creeds made it sound like salvation—like trading your soul for someone else's life is noble. Beautiful. Holy."

The memories break through the surface and flood through my mind.

"It used to be about power, ego, money… whatever," I say, trying to calm my thoughts. "Now it's self righteousness wrapped up as sacrifice. They don't care about the cost if the outcome is one they desire. The problem isn't their soul. It's everything that they could have become snatched away to save someone who was meant to die."

Julian leans forward, voice low. "How do you know all this?"

I don't answer right away. Instead, I look across the room—toward Theron. The love of my life. My soulmate.

His eyes meet mine, and they're sad. Not because he disagrees—he remembers.

He's the only one who was with me during the end of life as I knew it.

"Because I know what it means to trade yourself for someone else—they called it witchcraft, but I called it love."

Salem, 1692

Chapter One

SELENE

I can hear the weeping before I even step through the door. My father, Issac, he's saying goodbye. My heart cracks at the sound of despair leaking through his voice.

My little sister is ill.

The village will call it a wasting sickness—divine punishment, maybe. It'll be witchcraft, if they get cruel.

But I know better. It's the kind of disease that drains slowly. Leaves her skin pale, her breath thin, her night-clothes damp with sweat from a fever no prayer can break.

They'll say it's God's will.

But I don't worship gods that let girls die like that.

I walk into the back room and see my father crying over her, holding her hand tenderly in his large, calloused ones. Mercy barely twitches beneath the blankets. She turns her pale face to me and licks her cracked lips. She smiles—just barely.

Her hair has come loose. It's always pulled back into a plait. She always loved doing it every day. Now she just doesn't have the strength. Instead of the vibrant volume she used to infuse it with, it just lays limply on her back.

This is not how she should be in her sixteenth year.

"Selene," my father says, moving away from the bed, letting me slide in next to her.

She's so small now. Her body—once full of boundless energy, always bustling with chores or humming a hymn—has gone still in the worst way. Almost like her body is waiting or her to realize it's time to go.

I kneel, placing the small vial in my palm. The amber liquid peeking through the frosted glass.

"You brought it?" Mercy whispers, her voice thin as a spider's thread.

"Of course I did." I brush a damp curl from her temple. "Stole it from the Widow Ames's cupboard while she was in church. Almost got smited on the spot."

Mercy huffs something that might be a laugh—or a breath caught wrong.

"You shouldn't steal," she says, but she's already reaching for the spoon I've filled.

"You shouldn't die," I murmur back, holding it to her lips. "Let's both work on being better."

She swallows slowly, grimacing as the bitterness hits. "Is it witch's brew?"

"No," I say, giving her a grin, or at least trying to, "just herbs and vinegar and prayers I mutter under my breath."

Her eyes flutter closed again, lashes ghosting over pale cheeks.

"You pray now?"

"Only when I'm desperate." I'm trying to keep the dread, the devastation from my voice. My mind refuses to believe this is it for her.

She nods, barely. "You must really love me."

I stare at her—my sister, my shadow. The only thing in this house that ever made it feel like home. My father and I don't have to say it. We've always known.

My chest tightens. "Desperation makes saints of all of us," I whisper. "Even me."

This medicine will help for now… but it won't stop the inevitable.

Mercy falls back into a peaceful sleep and I brush her hair off of her forehead. The tears won't fall, not yet. Still, she's *dying* and there's nothing anyone can do about it.

"Selene." I turn to see my father behind me. He has tears in his gray eyes. "I would like to speak to you."

I give Mercy a kiss on her forehead and follow my father out of the room. His hands are weathered from years of carpentry. His face is weathered with the stress of losing his daughter.

We already lost my mother. She died giving birth to Mercy, she bled out in the very bedroom her daughter now lay in.

"Pastor Crowe has asked for your hand in marriage." Obadiah Crowe. Head pastor. Saint by title, serpent by soul. Revered by the town. Feared by every woman who's ever dared to speak.

If the Devil wanted a vessel, he wouldn't need to build one—he'd wear Obadiah's skin like a glove. No one would be able to tell the difference.

This isn't the first time he's asked for my hand. Each time, my father said no. That alone made us a curiosity. Refusing a man like Obadiah? In a town like this? Unheard of.

We played it off, telling him and everyone who asked that he could have anyone. That I would hate to deny another woman of the honor.

But I always knew the truth. He wanted the one woman he couldn't tame. That woman just so happens to be me.

"I've decided to accept his proposal," Isaac continues.

My heart stutters to a halt. He would never. "You would give me to *him*?"

He flinches, but doesn't answer.

"Why now?" My voice shakes. I don't try to control the rage in my tone. This deserves my anger. *How could he?*

My father sighs and turns around. He can't even look me in the eye. That's how I know that the decision has been made.

"Pastor told me that he can cure Mercy." *Of course, he did.*

"He's lying and you know it!" I'm shouting like a child, I know that. But there's no chance that he can do that, he wouldn't even if he could.

"Maybe," my father says. "But what if he isn't? What if he can save my daughter."

His daughter. That's the crux of it. Mercy is his blood. I am nothing to him but a way to save her.

I was given to him—placed in his and my late mother's care by the Church when I was barely old enough to walk. So of course he'd trade me to save her.

I'm not his daughter. I'm his burden.

My father may not care, but he is a man of a false god. Time for him to pay too. "You've damned me to save her."

He doesn't deny it. I may love Mercy. More than life itself. She deserves a life, but do I deserve one less?

I look my father in the eye. I can see him begin to shake with anger. He didn't think this would be easy. He thought I'd fight and then conform. He is very wrong.

"But I will not marry Obadiah Crowe."

I walk away without another word. She needs help. But Obadiah will never be able to cure the incurable. And no cure is worth what he'll do to me.

There is a knock on the door. My heart stills to a complete stop. My world is about to shift. And not in a good way. Isaac pushes past me to answer it.

"You will marry Pastor Crowe," he whispers sharply. "He is here to collect what is his."

The smile on his face turns evil. It's the kind of smile men wear when they think God is on their side. The devil incarnate has already entered the room.

My father opens the door before the second knock. "Pastor," he says, his voice that of the perfect host, stepping aside. "Right on time."

Obadiah Crowe steps into the house like it's already his. He removes his hat with exaggerated grace, tucking it beneath his arm before dipping his head to Isaac—pretending deference in a place he doesn't belong. His coat is finer than anyone else's in town, black wool trimmed with silver at the cuffs, a chain cross gleaming on his chest.

His blue gaze looks around the room until it finds mine. Cold as the river in midwinter. "God bless this house," he says, "and the women within it."

I don't respond. I've seen how the town adores him. The women stop singing and bow their heads to the God that is entering their line of sight. How men stumble over their own words just to earn his approval. He speaks, and they call it prophecy. He threatens, and they call it scripture.

But I see the truth. I always have. When he looks at me, there's nothing godly behind his eyes. Everyone seems to forget what happened to his first wife. Or maybe they just choose to pretend it didn't happen that way. All that piety —just enough to bury a grave.

"Don't pretend you've ever blessed anything in your life," I say.

"She's still full of spirit," he says to my father, like I'm not in the room. "But that can be tempered."

My hands curl into fists.

My father doesn't hesitate. "We've spoken," he says. "Mercy's recovery is proof enough. The pastor's faith has brought us favor. This is the path forward."

"No," I snap. "It's a deal. Yours and his."

Obadiah steps closer, folding his hands like he's about to deliver a sermon.

"I've prayed for you, Selene. For your pride to be humbled. For your defiance to bow to grace."

"You prayed for your own desires," I say, keeping my voice low. I don't want to wake Mercy. "Without even caring about mine."

He smiles wider. "I prayed for obedience. And now I offer you salvation through union. A pastor's house. A place at my side."

My stomach turns. "You mean a prison."

"A sanctified union," he says, smile never slipping.

"I will not marry you." I would rather die than spend even one night alone with him.

His smile drops. He wasn't expecting that. He should have

"You will," my father says, tone like stone. "You'll do what's right. For Mercy. For this family."

"Don't talk to me about family." I spit the words out. "Mercy is your daughter. I'm just the girl the church left on your doorstep," I take a step closer to him. "You're selling me to save her. You know that's what you're doing."1692

"You never belonged in this house," he says as he shoves me into Obadiah's waiting arms. "The Church forced you on us. We took you in when no one else would. And now you can be returned to them. Our debt is paid."

Obadiah grabs my arm and pulls me to the town square. The square hums with hymns.

Bodies fill every inch—pressed shoulder to shoulder like sheep herded to witness salvation or slaughter, no one quite sure which. The gallows loom at the center, built to withstand anything that comes its way. A reminder of what happens when people fall out of line.

Women scream prayers. Men watch like judges. Children sit cross legged in the mud, told to stay quiet, to stay still, to watch and learn. All of them facing forward. All of them singing.

Someone sees us. People notice and all stand. Heads turn. Eyes track our slow approach.

Obadiah walks in front, his black robes billowing in the wind, expression calm and devout. My father follows, jaw set, eyes dry. I walk between them. Wrists still in the Pastor's hands. I keep my spine straight and steps even.

The crowd parts like we are holy. Some bow their heads. Others reach out, brushing their fingers against the hem of Obadiah's sleeve like it'll bless them.

Pastor Crowe stands at the center of the altar that he had built for himself, one hand raised like he's calling down heaven itself.

"God has shown His favor," he declares, voice booming across the crowd. "A union sanctified by His hand—Selene Winscott, chosen for my household." Applause breaks through the crowd. The pastor's voice booms across them. "This union is God's plan," he says, "crafted for greatness. A vessel refined."

A widow wipes her tears and smiles through them. A girl clutching her mother's hand stares at me with envy. A man mutters to his companion. "But she's far past the usual match for someone as exalted as the pastor."

Obadiah steps forward, arms open. "You may ask why I chose her," he says. He paces slowly around the pulpit. "Not for her youth. Not for ease. But for her mind. Her spirit. She's unafraid. She's seasoned. She knows her worth."

A ripple of uneasy approval spreads through the crowd. They want assurance—heavenly logic for a match that feels wrong to several. He leans down to whisper a final word I can't hear over the drums of expectation.

He inclines his head toward me. "Come forward."

I do what he says with my chin held high. The rope of my bodice feels tighter than it should, the air too thin, but I don't waver.

"I will not marry you," I say. I did not whisper it. I declared it loud enough for all to hear. Isaac gets an onslaught of stares but he keeps his angry eyes on me.

There are gasps and murmurs. Even the crows seem to pause on the steeple. No one expected someone to reject the most powerful man in town.

Pastor Crowe's smile doesn't falter, but it starts to fracture. Piece by piece. The corners of his lips tremble like a mask slipping.

"You will mind your tongue," he murmurs, low enough for only me to hear. "The Lord hears."

"Then let Him," I whisper back. "Let Him see who you are when the crowd stops watching."

His hand clamps around my arm—tight, possessive, practiced. The crowd erupts again, mistaking it for affection, for holy restraint. Women sigh. Men nod. The pastor beams his smile as false as the god he claims to serve and says, "The Lord tests all wills, but love shall triumph."

The crowd cheers. I let them. Let them think they've witnessed devotion.

But when he leans close, his breath is hot against my ear.

"You'll regret this," he says, still smiling for the masses. "The Lord may forgive rebellion. I do not."

I meet his gaze, unflinching. "Good. I wasn't asking for your forgiveness."

He squeezes harder. His nails, long from the lack of any real labor, bite through the fabric of my sleeve. The applause drowns the sound of it. To them, it's a holy moment. To me, it's the first ring of a noose tightening.

When he leads me away, they don't see the bruise already forming beneath his fingers. They only see a shepherd guiding his lamb. And no one in Salem ever questions the shepherd.

He doesn't speak as he shuts the door to his house behind us. He walks past me like he's praying for patience.

"You embarrassed me," he says, his jaw clenched and tight. "In front of the town. In front of *God*."

I don't flinch. "Good."

"You think you're righteous?" His voice cracks in anger. "You think defiance is holy? That pride will save you when judgment comes?"

I lift my chin. "I think your God wouldn't need chains to earn worship."

His hands twitch. Just barely. But I see it. He steps closer. "You'll be silent. You'll be *still*. You'll learn obedience if I have to carve it into your bones."

I take a step closer, a smile creeping across my lips. "Try."

His eyes narrow. Then the mask of holiness drops completely. It's not the bravest thing I've ever done, but it's up there. And I'm proud.

I can almost see the sermon forming behind his eyes, his lips pressed into a flat, ecclesiastical disgust. He steps closer, the boards sigh under his weight. There's an instant where I think he'll go for the collar, drag me down by the nape, but he doesn't want to touch me with anything that gentle.

Instead, he pulls his arm all the way back, letting his palm collide with the side of my face.

My cheekbones go numb, then burn. There's a momentary delay between the strike and the heat crawling up my face, like the neurons need a moment to calibrate the pain.

My head jerks to the left. A smear of saliva splashes onto my tongue with the copper taste of blood. I keep my feet. I will not stagger, not for him. The room is bright, full of gnats of light. For a second, I can't hear anything.

When the hum dies, Obadiah is closer, and I can smell him—palm soap, bitter tea, and the faintest echo of herbal aftershave, the kind he had to have bought, not made. I look back at him, making a point of locking my eyes to his. My vision doubles at the edges but I keep the target.

He raises his hand again, but this time it closes on my throat.

His palm covers half my neck, his thumb slides into the angle of my jaw, squeezing until I feel the pulse start to hammer up against it. The fingers squeeze until the vertebrae creak. I try to draw a breath, but it catches behind the blockade of his grip.

He drags me forward, backward, into the air or the wall or nothing at all. My toes scrabble for purchase on the floorboards, but he has me fully extended, arms locked.

My arms come up, automatic, to pry at his wrist, but I know even as I do it that I haven't got leverage. My fingernails drag down his skin, but he does not register the pain. He is past pain now. He is a conduit for something else. Or maybe someone else.

There's a sound I make. Everything else is compressed into a single needlepoint of pressure and heat at the center of my neck. My eyes water. I look at him and see, briefly, that he's smiling—not with pleasure, but with the bleak certainty of a man fulfilling a promise.

The sound of my heartbeat is so loud it feels like it should be audible outside my body.

Black edges begin to bite into the periphery of my vision. There's a moment where I realize that this isn't theatre, this isn't a game, that he is going to do it, he is going to snuff me out here and now.

"I have no problem killing you and calling it an accident," he spews. "I have done it before, and I will do it again. For your insolence."

I think of defiance, I think of knives, I think of fire and salt. I think of how stupid it would be to die here, now, with his name the last word in my mouth.

He drags me to the bedroom by my hair. The feeling of the splintering wood under my palms. He throws me onto his bed, letting me lay there to rot.

"I will return when you learn your place," he says. Then he slams the door shut, clicking the lock. I don't know how long I lay there, half curled on the bed of a house that reeks of oil and dust.

I sit up and hobble to the door. It doesn't matter what Obadiah Crowe says or does.

That bastard will *never* own me.

SELENE

I will never bind myself to Obadiah. He may believe himself the voice of the Lord. But he's nothing more than a false prophet.

I may not be powerful. I am an orphan that was never claimed. Still, it's better to walk alone than lie beside one who would rot the soul from within.

I push myself off of the bed and limp to the window. My room is on the first floor. Providence aids the desperate.

The darkness has taken over the yard and far beyond. I shift to move the glass, but nothing happens. It's jammed or locked from the outside.

My only route of escape is stuck.

If I'm going to endure this, I'm going to need to deceive the good pastor like my life depends on it.

The door to the bedroom opens and I drop to my knees, pretending to be praying out the window.

"I see you've come to your senses," Obadiah says. I can hear the sneer in his voice.

"I have, Pastor," I say, turning to him. "I've decided my

sins are what is keeping me at bay. If it is permissible, may I visit the church?"

His smile lights up the room in a truly evil way. "You may, Selene. I was about to go there to work on my sermon. Would you like to accompany me?"

That was easier than I thought it was going to be. I guess his own ego controls him more than I believed it to be. "I would be honored to, pastor."

He helps me to the door like he wasn't the one to beat me to a pulp to begin with. His little soldiers surrounded the house. He, of course, speaks to them. "I will be taking my wife to the church to repent. Do not disturb us."

None of them flinch when they look at me. They're used to this level of violence. "Yes, pastor," they say in unison.

Then we're off. Though I have not claimed belief in the Almighty, I hope He hears me now. I need all the assistance I can get.

The pastor's house speaks of worldly gain, but the church bears the plainness of the people that live in the town.

The wind slips through the cracks in the timber walls, moaning like the ghosts of the damned. It howls down the aisle, rattling loose boards and whispering secrets through the pews—the kind of cries that sound too human to be just wind.

Obadiah leads us to his office, but if I want to visit the library. I need to seek a glimmer of hope. Of anything. I must act now.

"Pastor…" I trail off, bowing my head to him.

"Yes, my wife."

"Might I visit the library?"

He scoffs, looking at me with so much disgust, I have

to pull my eyes away. I need to be careful not to say anything unseemly.

"I only meant... I overheard you quoting the Book of Tobit last Sunday, and I did not know the story. I wished only to read it so I might better serve you. That I might speak thy name with honor when I walk among the wives."

He walks us towards the altar. "You wish to read the works to understand the words I say? I can agree to that."

Hope flared to life in my chest, before it was doused like a bucket of water over a small flame. "But you will read the works I give you. You will not wander. And you will repeat what you read to me so I know that it has taken root. Do you understand?"

He gives me a look of such love that an ordinary woman may believe it. Not me. I know what it is. His ego has worked its way through the narrative. As it always does.

"That is all that I could ever ask for," I say leaning up to give him a chaste kiss on the cheek, trying to swallow the sickness that rose within me.

I walk to the library on my own with the key that he gave me. It's in the back room of the church. One only the pastor has access to.

The walls are filled with bookshelves—all containing books of destruction and justification. Leather bound bibles everywhere.

The floor creaks as I walk across. So much knowledge locked away from prying eyes.

I drag my hand along the spines, looking for the book that can save my sister. I sit on the floor, pull out my journal, and begin to write.

The 5th day of the 11th Month, 1692

Isaac says that if I take Obadiah's hand in marriage, Mercy's soul may yet be spared. He speaks as though God Himself has declared it so.

But my heart knows another truth. If Obadiah were a man of salvation, Mercy would not be suffering now.

There must be another way to keep her from death. I cannot believe that God grants only one path, and that it must be through him.

These books—locked away, hidden from women—they hold knowledge I was never meant to see. Yet here I read, and here I feel hope stir.

I am not helpless. I will not surrender her.

If there is a way to save Mercy, I will find it. Even if it costs my life.

Obadiah is giving me until dawn. He will finish his sermon by then and our wedding will commence. I have until then to find the answers I seek.

I search for hours and find nothing. Each shelf, each corner, turns up more of the same.

That is until a book falls from the highest shelf, the one that I can't reach.

It lands with a heavy thud. I crawl over to it, ignoring the pain from my earlier beating.

The cover is dark. Almost black. Running my hand over it, I can't tell what this material is. Not leather.

Almost flesh like pulled over a book that was cured badly. It's stitched together with wax thread that's gone yellow.

There's no title on the front. Only a symbol burned into the center—a circle with a broken eye and some kind of star looking image.

I flip it over and suddenly, I feel the wind push my hair back and something in my chest lights up.

The pages inside are thick. They're not parchment—something else. There isn't ink in the normal sense. It's raised along the wording… like a brand.

It's in latin… the words.

Sanguine ligatur, dolore aperitur. Non tu daemonem vocas—te daemon vocavit. Pro carnis pretio, libertas datur.

"It is bound by blood, opened by pain," I whisper. "You do not summon the demon—the demon summoned you. For the price of flesh, freedom is given."

I stare at the page, heart pounding. The directions tell me exactly what's expected. They call upon me to do the unthinkable. To summon a demon from the Pit.

I don't know what I'm doing. But I have nothing to lose. And I need someone—anyone—to listen.

Even if what hears me comes from Hell. It's a chance I'm willing to take

I find some charcoal in the basket in the corner of the room. Ironic that I'm using what the children use to draw.

I place the book at the center of the room, push the tables aside, and begin. Line after line. Curves and knots. Circles that close in on themselves.

When the last symbol is drawn, I reach for the pin at my collar. When I press it to my palm, I don't feel any pain. Three drops of blood fall into the bowl at the center of the floor.

I unclasp the locket from my neck. The last thing I have of my birth mother. And I place it beside the blood.

"Let this be the cost," I whisper.

I look into the book and see the words that I need to say to call forth a demon. "I call to the ones who walk between shadow and flame. Let one who would bargain step forth."

Flames rise from the floor and lick up to the ceiling, their heat pulses outward, but it doesn't scorch my skin. The circle glows, the blood boiling at its center. Shadows twist along the walls, bending in ways they shouldn't.

Something steps through the fire door.

He is tall, impossibly so, with edges that flicker like candlelight. Eyes like embers. A voice that hums through the bones of the room, though he hasn't spoken.

I can't move. I'm not sure if it's due to the fact that I'm terrified… or if he has power that has me frozen in place.

"You called," he says, voice low as prayer. "And I—Cassian—have answered."

His gaze shifts to the blood, then to the locket. One brow lifts, not in mockery, but in interest.

"You gave of yourself. Not common, not for a first calling."

"I didn't know what would come," I whisper.

"You still do not." He steps closer, fire curling at his feet as he crosses the circle.

"So, then," he says. "What is it you seek, little heretic?"

I gather my breath. "Her name is Mercy. My sister. She is struck with fever. Her body weakens. He—"

I lower my eyes. "The pastor claims he can save her, but his mouth is full of dust and lies. He watches her fade, while he plays prophet."

"You do not ask for healing," he says. "You seek deliverance."

"Not for me," I say. "For her. Mercy deserves to have a life that is not full of strife or cut short."

"And what would you give, to steal her back from the grave?"

"My blood. My name. My loyalty. Whatever price you name, I will pay it—so long as she lives."

He studies me, long and still. The kind of silence that feels like judgment.

"These are my terms," he says. "Your life is your own… for a time. But when I call, you will come. You will not flee, nor hide, nor deny me. You will stand at my side and serve as I require."

"And in return?" I breathe.

"She lives," he says, the words falling heavy as stone. "Her fever breaks at dawn's first light."

"Swear it."

"By ash and shadow. By fire, and by the thread of fate —I swear it." His eyes show it all. He's not lying to me.

The circle glows a shade of crimson and gold, just once. With the fading light, the blood vanishes and the locket flies to my hand. Then I feel it—the bond. It latches to something inside me. A thread pulled taut.

Cassian raises his hand. Out of nowhere, a scroll unfurls from the air itself—parchment aged and darkened at the edges, its seal bound in black wax, stamped with a mark I don't recognize. The symbol flickers, shifting as though alive.

"Every oath must be witnessed," he says. "Every soul that bargains must bind it in blood."

Cassian produces a quill—its tip glinting like a fang.

I take it, prick my finger, and press it to the page. My

blood moves across the parchment like it knows the way. My name appears, one letter at a time, drawn out as though the scroll remembers me like an old friend.

When the final stroke settles, the wax seal re-forms and closes with a hiss of smoke.

Cassian takes the scroll and it disappears into flame.

"It is done," he says. "Sealed in word. Sealed in blood."

"She will live?" I ask again.

"You have bought her more than life," he replies. "You've bought her time. And now, I own your soul."

He turns toward the heart of the circle. The flames rise once more, and for a moment, he is little more than shadow and fire.

"Our bond is sealed," he says. "When the hour comes… I shall find you."

Then he's gone. As quickly as he came.

The door crashes open, striking the wall with a crack. A woman stands in the threshold. A patron. Dawn spills through the doorway behind her, gilding the room in pale light. All that runs through my mind is Mercy.

She looks around—at the marks on the floor, the bowl, the blood, the ash. At me.

Her scream pierces through the library. "A witch!" she cries. "There is a witch here!"

Obadiah steps up behind her, like he was following her down here. His shadow stretches long in the morning light, an omen that speaks of nothing but pain and suffering.

One look at his face, and I know.

He saw.

"You were not meant to do that, Selene," he says, his voice deadly low.

And he is angrier than I have ever seen him.

Not meant to do that. He knows something about what happened, on a deeper level than he's meant to. I don't get a chance to ask him.

"Arrest her," he continues. "She belongs in the cells below us. A trial will commence against these heinous acts."

Seems like Cassian is about to get my soul before he is expecting.

Chapter Three

SELENE

They buried me beneath the altar.

Just rough hands, even rougher stone, and the echo of Obadiah's footsteps as the door slammed shut above me.

The cell is cold. Damp stone lines the walls, black with mildew. Iron rings bolt into the corners, rusted and stained. There's no bed, no blanket, no light. Only straw and rot, and the distant weeping of someone I cannot see.

A holy prison, they call it. But there's nothing holy here. Only silence thick enough to drown in.

I sit with my back to the wall, hands aching where the ropes cut into my wrists. They didn't bother to wash the blood off. *Let it stay,* I think. *Let it stain.*

They want a confession.They want repentance.

They'll get neither.

Not when Mercy is alive above me, breathing freely for the first time in weeks. Not when the fire still smolders in my chest.

Not when the deal is sealed, and I can feel the thread—

still pulling, still tethered—between me and something far deeper than this cell.

Cassian's words echo in the quiet. *"When the hour comes… I shall find you."*

Let him come. Let them all come.

I have already traded my soul. What more can they take?

The days bleed together. I think it's been a week, but it's hard to tell when there are no windows. No sun. Only the scrape of the door above when they toss down a crust of bread or a ladle of water.

No one dares to speak to me.

My body is giving in before my will. I feel it—how hard it is to sit up now. How my limbs tremble even when I'm still. My breath rattles in the cold, too loud in the silence.

They have not let me see Mercy.

That's the cruelest part. Not the hunger or the chill. The not knowing and waiting.

Did she ask for me? Or have they told her I'm evil and she made the choice to not see me?

I tried, once, to call up—screamed her name until my throat gave out. No one came.

Obadiah sent word three days ago. Or what I think was three days. His message came through a guard with a voice like gravel and a sneer to match.

"Your trial is set. The people will gather. The pastor will speak."

They say it like scripture. As if the outcome is already written.

Isaac has not come.

Not once. Not a glance. Not a word.

I knew he didn't love me—but now I know he truly

never wanted me. The message he sent was simple, signed in another's hand.

You are no daughter of mine.

The lock turns. The iron door groans open.

I don't move. Just blink into the dark as the sound of boots echo down the stone steps.

Obadiah.

His silhouette fills the frame. The door slams behind him, sealing us in.

"So quiet now," he says, voice soft. "No sermons from the mouth of the heretic?"

I stare at the floor. I won't give him the satisfaction.

He takes a step closer. "I trusted you. I offered you the sanctity of my name. A place in my house. And this… this is how you repay me? With devils? With blasphemy?"

Still, I do not speak.

His hand moves faster than I can track—a sharp crack across my face. My head snaps sideways, cheek blazing.

I taste blood. The second blow comes like thunder—a fist this time, straight to my ribs. I crumple forward, gasping.

"You were supposed to be a wife," he growls. "A mother. A vessel for God's will."

I lift my chin, mouth already thick with blood. My lip is split, my breath uneven.

"You mean *your* will," I rasp.

Another blow. Stars flash to life behind my eyes and I fall to my knees. He leans in, hand tangled in my hair, and forces me to look up.

"You are nothing now, Selene. No family. No name. By this time tomorrow, you'll hang."

And that's when I spit in his face—a mouthful of blood and spite.

His whole body jerks back.

I drag myself upright, using the wall for balance. Every bone in me screams. My knees shake. But I stand.

"You can break my body," I say, voice low. "You can steal my name, chain my hands, starve me until there's nothing left—" I meet his eyes. "—but you will never destroy me."

Obadiah stares at me, fury etched into every line of his face. But beneath the rage… there's satisfaction.

"I should thank you," he says, voice low. "Mercy is healed. The fever broke just as the sun rose—exactly as you hoped."

My heart thunders. She lives.

He leans closer, a cruel smile tugging at his mouth. "The town rejoices me for it. They call it divine. *My* prayers, they say. *My* touch. They will never know the truth. Not of demons. Not of you. I will not let your name stain this town further."

I don't speak. I can't. My nails dig into my palms. I want to tear the smile from his face.

"They will never know what you gave," he says, a mockery of kindness. "Because I am merciful."

He turns from me without another word, cloak brushing the stone.

But I spit one more time—blood and defiance. He flinches.

"You can bury me," I say, voice ragged. "But fire always finds its way back to air."

His jaw tightens as he ascends the stairs, slow and steady.

The iron door slams. The lock clicks home.

I am alone again—bruised, bleeding, and unbroken.

They come for me at dawn. There are two guards this time, their faces grim, hands rough as they grab ahold of my bare arms.

They untie me from the wall and drag me up the stairs. My legs barely hold. My mouth is dry, split and bloodless. Still, I walk.

I will not crawl. Not for them.

Outside the cell, the church is alive with voices, humming like a hive. The town has gathered. I hear the creak of pews. The scrape of boots on timber. And the bells —three solemn tolls—to mark the opening of the trial.

They march me through the main aisle. My funeral awaits.

Faces blur past me, but I know them. I know all of them.

Goody Whitlow, who held my hand when I scraped my knee as a child, now glares at me like I've spat on her doorstep. Elijah Carter, who once gave me apples in the autumn, refuses to meet my eyes. The woman who sold me my thread, the boy who danced with me at midsummer, the midwife who held me at birth. They're all here. And they hate me.

I raise my head, searching the pews.

Mercy. Wrapped in a shawl, hair still damp from the rain , but eyes clear. She clutches the edge of the pew, knuckles white. She looks at me—then quickly looks away.

My heart sinks to my feet.

She's alive. But she won't meet my gaze.

Isaac is beside her, his arm around her like she's a fragile thing. His face is carved from granite. He doesn't even scowl. He looks at me like I am already dead.

The guards shove me to the front and force me to my knees on the planks beneath the pulpit. My hands are bound again. I feel the tremble in my limbs, but I hold myself still.

Obadiah stands behind the altar like a judge robed in black, though he wears only his usual sermon coat. A Bible lies open before him.

He raises his voice.

"Let it be known," he calls, "that on this day, before God and men, we try this woman—Selene Winscott, betrothed in name but not in spirit—for the crime of witchcraft and consorting with infernal powers."

The crowd murmurs. A few clutch their crucifixes.

"She stands accused of violating sacred space, invoking unholy spirits, corrupting the name of God, and drawing on power that is not her own."

He looks to the crowd, letting their murmurs linger.

"We have seen the signs. Heard the testimony from the witness. Feel the blight of her presence." He looks down at me. "Do you deny the charge?"

I lift my chin. "I do."

A few gasp. A child whimpers.

"I saved Mercy," I say, voice hoarse, but as loud as I can make it. "No one else. I gave everything for her—and you took it."

Obadiah's lip curls. "You confess, then, to making a deal with a devil."

"I confess to doing what you could not."

He slams a hand against the pulpit. "You dare speak in defiance before your town? Before your God?"

"This town turned its back on me the moment you opened your mouth," I say. "And your God? If He would rather let an innocent girl die than hear a woman speak—then He is no god of mine."

The church erupts in shouts. Words like "heretic", "whore", and "Jezebel" fly from the pews.

Obadiah raises his hand. The room comes to a halt. He turns to the town. "You have heard her words. You have seen her unrepentant heart. She names herself."

The elders at the side—men with parchment and pens—nod in solemn agreement.

"We will proceed to the final stage. She shall be taken to the gallows at dawn. That her soul might be judged by fire, and her name purged from our records."

I stare at the rafters above me. There are scorch marks there.

Let them try.

The guards don't speak. They drag me down the steps by my arms, throw me like a sack of grain into the stone pit, and slam the door above.

My knees hit the floor. I stay there, hunched, breath shivering through cracked lips. My hands tremble in my lap, bones bruised, skin torn where the ropes rubbed raw.

They say I'll hang at dawn.

I close my eyes.

My thoughts stretch toward the tether I still feel buried in my chest. That thin, burning line connecting me to something that I know is watching.

Cassian said that he would come when it is my time. It seems I will be seeing him sooner than I expected.

I open my eyes.

Lying before me on the stone floor is a piece of parchment. A quill beside it, long and black as night.

I know it. I've seen it before—when I signed the pact in blood.

My hand moves before I can stop it. I reach for the quill.

There's no ink.

I press it to the tip of my finger and wince as it draws a single drop of blood. It beads up, warm and bright in the dark.

I write a message to Cassian across the parchment.

My soul is yours... sooner than you think.

The blood dries instantly. The letters glow faintly, like embers.

I crawl to the tiny iron brazier in the corner—the only light the cell has known. A low flame flickers within, barely holding on.

I hold the parchment above it.

For a moment, nothing happens.

Then the paper curls and vanishes in a pulse of ash and heat, as if swallowed whole.

I'm left alone again.

The darkness settles all around me.

But I feel him.

Somewhere beyond the veil—I know he's listening.

THERON

My father has returned from another deal. He's in the study, sifting through names—souls marked, bargains made, those whose time is drawing near.

Cassian Duvain. The one even demons whisper about.

And Serenya, my mother. Grace and flame in equal measure.

Together, they are the heart of this house—the spine and soul of everything I know. They raised Evander and me. Evander is my brother. We're thick as thieves.

In this realm where blood seals pacts and names hold power, they were our first shelter. Our fiercest teachers. Our truest home.

Cassian lounges in a high-backed chair near the scroll table, reading over death warrants and the desperate promises scrawled beneath them. Serenya stands by the hearth, draped in obsidian silk, sipping from a goblet that catches the glow of the coals.

She doesn't look up when she speaks.

"You've been down here for too long," Serenya says,

her voice velvet edged. "When will you walk the mortal world again?"

Cassian chuckles low. "We've just returned, my heart. Let the ink dry."

"That wasn't walking," she replies. "That was work. There's no pleasure in closing someone else's contract."

My mother stands by the fire, the light curling around her like it remembers her before it became flame. She turns, eyes finding mine. She's never been soft, but will hold your hand through darkness and drags you through it, if she must. "You sit in this house awaiting your future like it will come to you."

Cassian chuckles behind his wine. "You're in one of your moods."

She smiles faintly, but her eyes are fixed on Theron and I. "I'm being your mother. That's always a dangerous thing."

She moves toward the scroll table, fingers brushing the edge of a parchment. I watch her—grace incarnate. "You were born with flame in your blood," she says. "But fire alone is not power. Even fire forgets it once was light."

I shift in my chair, uneasy. "You want us to go into the mortal world. To... what? Snatch someone from the first village we pass through?"

"No," she says simply. "I want you to see. To look long enough to recognize what fate has already placed at your feet."

She looks at me, and it's like being seen from the inside out.

"She lit the circle like a matchstick and offered blood and sentiment. What kind of man would I be if I didn't show up for something so... intoxicating?"

Serenya arches a brow as she turns to face Cassian.

"I think," Serenya says, stepping closer to him, "you've been marked. Whether you admit it or not."

"He's not ready," Cassian says.

"Neither were you," she says, brushing her hand across his shoulder as she passes. "But I loved you before you knew your own name."

I can't respond. Not before the fire explodes out of the fireplace.

The flames rise. Heat pulses through the room, and a spray of ash spits from the hearth, scattering across the stone.

From the heart of the fire, something forms. Paper. Curling out of the flame like it's being formed by the smoke.

My father reaches forward without flinching. The scroll lands neatly in his hand, still warm.

He turns it over once. His face is unreadable as he reads it. "My soul is yours… sooner than you think."

The letters glow like they've been seared into flesh.

But I feel it. Whatever thread she just pulled, it doesn't wrap around just my father.

It hums in the blood. It stirs something in me I cannot name. As if a voice I've never heard is whispering in the marrow of my bones.

"She calls," my mother says behind us, voice low. "And not just with words."

She steps closer, gaze moving from Cassian to me. Serenya rests a hand on my chest, just over my heart. "Some souls know each other before the world does," she whispers. "Sometimes the blood remembers before the mind understands."

Cassian's jaw flexes once.

"I need to go," he says, low. "And I need your help."

That alone means something's wrong. *He never asks.*

"She made a deal. And her time—" He stops, teeth clenching. "—her time's almost gone."

That shouldn't be possible. I know it. *He* knows it. When demons strike a bargain, it stays that way until the soul is ready to be collected and never before.

Unless someone's broken it.

"Mortals interfered," he adds, voice showing his ancient anger. He hates when mortals interfere. "They think they can rewrite fate."

He finally looks at us.

"Her name is Selene Winscott."

A name I don't know—but my body reacts before my mind does. That thread again. Tighter. Burning behind my ribs.

Mother's breath catches like she's seen this before.

"You felt her," she says, not a question. Not to Evander, but directly to me.

Cassian says nothing. That silence is its own confession.

Father doesn't blink. "Then we go. Now."

I nod. It doesn't matter that I don't understand. I've *never* been more certain we're already too late. Yet hoping we aren't.

All four of us. Into the breach. Into whatever storm dares pull a soul out from under Cassian Duvain's hand.

Salem is wet with fog, the ground slick with rot. There's smoke in the wind. Not the same as what we have in Hell.

This one smells of mortal fear and desperation wrapped in a box and tied together with a bow.

We arrive just outside the edge of the village. The trees are bare and the first signs of the winter season are in the land. The magic coils around us like shadow, cloaking what shouldn't be here.

Evander is standing next to our father. Like me, he looks around at our surroundings. We're rarely ever in the mortal world, both of us preferring to stay away from humans at all cost.

My mother wraps her arm around me and squeezes my shoulder.

Selene Winscott. Whoever she is... she shouldn't be dying.

We reach the church in moments. Cassian doesn't knock—he touches the door and it splits at the hinges.

Inside, the chapel is still. Dead still. The pews don't creak. The wind doesn't move. It's so quiet in here that I'm worried if we're too late.

We descend below.

The door to the cell hangs loose on one hinge. Bent at the lock, like it tried to hold her and failed.

We step inside. There's no chains, no body. Only blood, a lot of blood. Slick and black where it pools. Sticky where it streaks. It paints the floor in two wide arcs—wide enough for a body to thrash.

A drag trail cuts through the center. One heel, then the other. It looks like it was just dead weight pulled across the stone. Palm smears break the line—fingers clawing for grip, slipping.

Cassian halts in the doorway. His shoulders don't move. His fists tighten. Serenya kneels beside the longest streak. Her fingers touch the stone. She tilts her head like she's listening to what it says. The blood glistens on her skin.

For one breathless moment, the cell is no longer empty.

Chains rattle. A scream cuts through the dark. A body dragged, fighting. The mark on the wall pressed deep in real time.

I *see* her. Held down. Stripped of even dignity. Her voice hoarse, mouth still forming the shape of *no*.

The vision dies. The stillness returns. Serenya lowers her hand."Where is she?" My father grounds out, pacing the cell like a rabid animal.

My mother steps to the center of the room, staring down at the blood in the circle. At the locket fragments still clinging to the edge. "They took her."

Cassian nods once. "And now they mean to kill her."

He turns toward the door. We hear it before we see it. Screaming. Feet pounding dirt. A voice shouting for silence. The cadence of a hanging.

Cassian stiffens beside me. "Move."

We cut through the village. Mortals part for us without knowing why. Their fear tastes like iron in the air.

She's being dragged toward the gallows. Dirt smeared across her face. Rope clutched in her fists like she can tear it apart with rage alone. She's snarling, screaming, still fighting even now.

I don't hear her voice. I feel it—ripping through me.

My left arm flares. It pulses and I stagger. Heat rolls through my chest like something *called,* and whatever it was, I've answered.

My vision tunnels. The world narrows until it's only her—only this girl who should be broken but refuses to fall.

Her gaze locks on mine. And that thread I've felt since

my father first said her name snaps tight. My lungs seize. My knees nearly give. Every part of my soul *recognizes her*. This isn't a coincidence.

It's fate.

The mark on my arm sears straight to the bone.

Not a signal.

A *claim*.

"Mate," I growl, the word dragging from deep in my chest—rough, primal, like it was branded there long before I ever saw her.

It doesn't feel like surrender.

It feels like I've been found.

Chapter Five

SELENE

It's the morning of the execution.

The cell has a chill pushing through it, but I don't feel the cold anymore. My body's gone past shivering, past aching. There's only numbness now. I have to accept my fate.

I sit on the stone floor with my spine against the wall, legs folded beneath me. My hands rest in my lap.

I'm not afraid.

I've done what I came to do. Mercy lives. That is my miracle.

And if this is the price—my blood for hers—then so be it. I'll pay it with my head held high.

For a long time, there is only silence. Then suddenly, I hear it. Footsteps.

They are above me. Moving the beams overhead and dropping dust in a cloud around me. They're coming.

Something in my chest tightens, just for a breath. Not out of fear or the instinct to live, but the thought of what the afterlife could be.

I close my eyes.

I do not pray.

I just breathe.

Let them come. Let them drag me out and call me a witch. Let the rope burn my flesh. Let the crowd cheer.

My soul is already gone. My choice has already been made.

And if death is the only honest thing left to me—I'll walk into it with my name still mine.

I can hear more steps. Walking down the stairs now. Coming to take me to my end.

I sit up straighter, though every joint screams. My fingers twitch with the need to brace for whatever or whoever I have to fight.

They've come to take me. I won't make it easy on them.

But when the door grinds open, it's not just the guards.

Obadiah steps in first, like always. Regal in his robes, eyes gleaming with victory. He looks straight at me like this is his ascension. Taking my life is his sermon. He thinks it earns him a place beside the Almighty—when truly, he's bound for a throne carved from flame.

Behind him is Isaac. His mouth is twisted in a smug curl. Not an ounce of grief in his eyes. Only satisfaction. He never has to claim me as his daughter again.

And Mercy.

She stands in a pale blue dress, cleaned and perfect. Her cheeks are flushed with health. Her hair is braided with ribbon. And she looks at me like she doesn't know me at all.

My stomach turns.

Obadiah stops in front of the cell, gripping the bars like a pulpit. "It is time," he says. "The people await justice."

"You were never meant to belong in my house," he spits. "Forced on us like a plague. The church gave us a curse when they gave us *you*. But now? Now that curse is lifted."

Mercy bites her lip, eyes darting from him to Obadiah.

Her voice is small, but it doesn't hold the same rasp of sickness as it did before. "He saved me."

My lungs halt. I don't move. The betrayal settles in my ribs like rotten flesh. I want to scream… but instead, I manage a small smile—not out of forgiveness, but because I'm done holding on to pretense that Mercy would make the right decision on who she would believe.

"Is that what you think?" My voice comes out hoarse, but enough to make her flinch. "You think *he* saved you?"

She falters, but doesn't speak. I rise slowly, using the wall to brace myself. The guards step closer. I don't care.

"I gave *everything* for you. My blood. My soul. My last breath. I made a deal with something no good soul should ever face. And you—" I look her dead in the eye. "You want to sing *his* praises?"

Mercy stares. Her lips part. But it's Isaac who interrupts.

"She lies. This is the devil's tongue, speaking through her."

But Mercy's gaze flickers. Her throat bobs. "I didn't ask you to do that," she snaps. "The pastor brought me light while you were always filled with darkness."

That's the last straw for me. The last bit of me that had any caring for anyone in my family. "No," I say. "You didn't. And if I had known what little love lived in you… I would've made a different bargain."

Mercy recoils like I slapped her. But I don't regret the words. Not one of them.

"You'll get your show," I say. "Hang me high. Praise your prophet. But you'll *never* be clean."

Obadiah looks too pleased—like a man who sees the board and knows the next move wins the game.

"Take her," he says.

The guards open the cell. I don't fight them. Let them drag me. I'm done kneeling. Or pretending.

They throw open the jail doors, and sunlight hits my face—the first I've seen in weeks.

I might've welcomed it once.

Now it only lights the path to my execution.

I don't walk to the gallows. They drag me.

My bare feet scrape stone. My body aches from where fists have landed and ribs have bruised. My wrists are bound so tightly the rope has worked its way into my skin. I don't flinch when they pull me down the street.

The townspeople are waiting. Rows of them. Standing in clusters along the dirt road. Children on shoulders. Women with handkerchiefs. Men who look hungry for a death that isn't theirs. They don't see a girl. They see a show.

Some whisper prayers. Others spit.

I keep my head high.

The gallows loom ahead, built atop Proctor's Ledge, where the trees break and the rock juts out like a broken tooth. There's no scaffold dressed in linen or ceremony here. Just a crude wooden frame hammered together towering over the ledge.

The platform is high, taller than a man. Wide enough for a single sinner. The ladder leans against it, splintered and crooked, each rung dark with weather and wear. A single beam stretches across the top like a cross laid on its side, and from it dangles the rope.

The noose hangs waiting.

The wood beneath it is stained. Not red anymore, but brown and deep—like the blood has soaked too far to ever wash away.

Obadiah ascends the platform beside the gallows that reaches up higher than the gallows. Robes trailing behind him like a holy man come to pass judgment. The sun catches on the silver at his throat, and he turns to face the crowd—hungry for salvation, or blood, or both.

He lifts his arms, and the crowd stills.

"The Devil's hold has grown bold," he proclaims, voice ringing out over the hill. "He walks among us, dressed in the flesh of our daughters. Tempts with lies. Corrupts with offers of assistance. But the Lord sees all."

He turns slightly, not looking at me—looking through me.

"This girl," he says, and the word *girl* curdles on his tongue, "gave herself to darkness. She whispered to depths of evil. Bartered her soul. Something that is sacred that only the Almighty can give. She claims it's for salvation for her sister, but *she* was the one who brought the sickness to the town with her wickedness."

Gasps ripple through the crowd as Obadiah points at me. A woman weeps. His eyes scan them, and his lips curl in satisfaction.

"But the Lord is just," he says. "And through His mercy, we are delivered. Today, this plague will be burned from our midst. And His light shall reign again."

He closes his Bible and he dips two fingers into a bowl of soot, and smears a single line across my brow.

"I act not for vengeance," he adds, softer now, almost gentle. "But obedience."

Then he gives a single nod—and the executioner steps forward like death called by name.

The rope is coarse against my neck as it's put on.

The executioner doesn't speak. Just pulls the knot tight, turns it once, and sets it high—behind the ear. The correct place. One that promises a quick death. No suffering. A grace they say I don't deserve.

I don't know if kindness lives here anymore.

My breath is shallow. My knees shake. But I do not cry.

Obadiah steps forward again, Bible clutched in one hand, the other raised as if to bless me.

"By law and scripture, you are offered final words, Selene Winscott," he says. "Speak, and let the Lord hear your repentance."

The crowd shifts, leans in, hungry.

He expects me to plead. To sob. To beg for forgiveness I don't owe.

But I lift my chin. "You built the gallows long before I ever sinned. Go on, then. Hang what you were always afraid of."

The rope bites against my neck. The wood creaks beneath my feet as I'm forced to the center. The platform feels smaller than I imagined. The sky is heavier.

Let it end. Let this be the last pain. The last moment of mortality I ever have to carry.

Obadiah's voice is somewhere behind me, all thunder and false righteousness. I don't hear the words.

My heart beats once as the lever pulls.

The world drops.

The noose tightens.

But the pain doesn't come.

Not in the way I expected. There's pressure. Crushing.

A scream locked in my throat. The world should go dark now. I *want* it to.

But it doesn't.

I try to breathe, thinking I'm suffocating. I can take in air. Something is wrong here.

In the space between breath and nothing, a hand closes around my wrist.

My body should be swinging—jerking—breaking. Instead, I'm weightless.

The rope still holds—but I do not fall.

My body dangles mid air, breath ragged, eyes wide. The world has gone silent—no gasp from the crowd, no rustle of wind.

Only the grip on my wrist, anchoring me to something I do not understand.

I look up.

A man—no, not just a man—stands atop the gallows, just below me. One hand grips my wrist, keeping me from the noose, from the drop, from the end.

His eyes catch the light—flecks of red and gold flickering like embers just before they blaze. His face is carved in something between fury and awe.

He isn't gasping, isn't trembling—but I feel the thrum of his pulse as if it beats in my own veins. Like he's tethered to something inside me.

And then it happens.

The pain.

It explodes beneath my skin—my left collarbone begins to sear white hot and painful. I scream. A mark blazes through my blood and then it fades just as quickly as it came.

But something remains.

A tether.

His hand grips my wrist, holding me suspended above death. The rope scrapes my throat, but it doesn't tighten. I don't fall. I just hang—dangling between one breath and the next.

The eyes. The fire. The inhuman strength.

"Gods' balls," I whisper.

Chapter Six

THERON

My grip on the woman's wrist never falters.

The rope is still wrapped around her neck—but I'll be damned if I let her fall.

Her time is not now.

A presence moves behind me.

"I got the hangman."

I turn around and see Evander standing there. Eyes blazing red as he steps up on the executioner, who is now cowering on the edge of the gallows. Whenever Evander takes a step forward, the executioner takes another back.

A man whose entire job is to end the lives of morals only to be petrified when faced with an immortal. Talk about poetic justice.

I take this moment to pull Selene to safety. Selene—my mate.

She's a fighter. I like that. Once she's standing on the platform, I tear the rope off her neck.

"Thank you," she says. No begging. No pleading for mercy. Just thank you for saving me. She doesn't fear me. I see her eyes. Her soul shines in her pupils. She holds my gaze without breaking the contact.

"You're mine," I say gravely. *That was the best that I could come up with?*

She steps back from me, a smirk forming at the edge of her lips. "We'll see."

She is going to be fun. I know it.

I look at Evander. He heard everything. He's smirking just like Selene. "Don't give in easily, sister," he says happily.

That bastard. For a moment, I forget we're surrounded. The crowd around us is shifting uncomfortably, though.

I let my power flow through me to listen to the words around me.

"She's a witch."

"Is that a sign that we're all doomed?"

"Is this some kind of curse?"

"Pastor will save us."

Pastor.

He's about to answer for almost killing my mate.

I hear singing. The songs of the crowd around us. I look out. They're scared. Not angry.

"Let not Thy servant fall to flame. For we are faithful, clean of name…"

Some people are furious. But most… they're hurting. They believe everything that the pastor says. They are looking for someone to tell them what to feel next. Sheep following a wolf and not a Shepard.

The singing gets louder and louder. The storm clouds seem to part.

They think it's the Almighty. I could tell them the science behind a storm. But they're not ready for that kind of knowledge yet.

The air parts like cloth. Smoke is curling like mist around the center of the stage. Shadows peel back bit by bit.

I help Selene down to the stage. My father is going to figure out what this pastor is up to and destroy him in the same breath.

Cassian steps through first. He may look calm, but he is the epitome of the calm before the storm. Not a sound follows his boots, but the wood beneath him groans all the same. His presence is a blade pressed to the world's throat.

And beside him—Serenya.

She's light and fury bound in one body. Hair like ink. Eyes like winter fire. Her skirts whisper across the platform, but even the wind dares not touch her. Where my father is power, my mother is the heart. They are one. And when they stand together—do not cross them.

Gasps ripple through the crowd. Someone drops to their knees. Someone else screams.

Cassian doesn't flinch.

His eyes sweep the people before they land on Selene. "She made a deal. And I always collect my debts. When they are due. She is not yet."

Obadiah stumbles back like he's been slapped. I *wish* he had.

"She was never yours to break," my mother says, her voice like silk soaked in blood. "She was marked by something older than your so called god."

Obadiah snarls. "You bring devils upon sacred ground—"

Cassian raises a single brow. "This ground was never sacred," he says, voice smooth. "It was soaked in lies before her blood ever touched it."

The crowd stirs. I turn to them, arm still around Selene.

Evander has joined us. The crowd begins to stir. Moving around, trying to figure out what is going on.

I feel Selene trembling beside me. Now this just won't do. Completely unacceptable.

Cassian steps forward, hands behind his back.

"The question isn't who she is," I say, stepping forward. "It's who you sold your soul to become."

Obadiah flinches. Ah I see he recognizes me now. He's not just a fraud. He's mine.

"You," I say aloud, leaning to get right in his face. "I remember you. You bartered with me once, didn't you?"

Cassian tilts his head. "He did."

My father would know. He signed off on the deal. In fact, it was one of my first deals. I remember everything about that night with Obadiah Crowe.

Man with no shoes or shirt. Cowering in the corner of an old abandoned building. Poor as dirt. "You traded your soul for power. For obedience. For the tongues of men and the title of pastor."

Selene turns. Her eyes lock on him. Obadiah doesn't meet them. I see all of the emotions pass through them.

"Hypocrite," she breathes. "You turned them against me—for sins you committed first."

I grab Selene's hand and look at her. She should know why Obadiah has been doing this whole thing.

"He's been killing those he calls witches," I say. "Trading their lives for time. A soul for a soul. The Devil's arithmetic. He chose women who dared to question him. The ones out there followed. But you—" I look at her beautiful face. "You were the kind of leader he could never become."

My mother chuckles like she's getting ready to celebrate the biggest party. "Time's up."

"No!" Obadiah shouts as he lunges straight for Selene.

Fool. I try to step in front of her but she doesn't retreat. She meets him halfway. Her fist cracks across his jaw. The sound of bone crunching like dry bark. Obadiah stumbles. Blood bursts from his mouth splattering his robes.

"Good thing you're wearing black," my mother mutters.

He growls something holy, but it dies under her next blow—a knee driven into his stomach so hard he gags. He's down on one knee, spitting blood out of his mouth. Selene grabs the front of his robes—the ones stitched with gold scripture—and rips.

"You preach with a serpent's tongue," she snarls, "but bleed like any mortal man."

He claws at her. She ducks, grabs his wrist, and twists until we hear the wet pop of a dislocated shoulder. His scream echoes through the square.

She slams him to the boards. His head hits the wood with a wet crack. Blood spreads beneath him, seeping between the holes.

Selene kneels over him. Her hand trembles, clenched in a fist above his throat. Her knuckles are raw, mouth set.

"You hung girls like me," she breathes. "Because you feared us."

He chokes out a cough. But his eyes won't meet hers. So she stands. Turns her back. Leaves him gasping in his own blood, broken on the wood.

"No," he whispers. "No—no, please. I served the light—"

"You served yourself," I counter him.

"I didn't know what I gave—"

I crouch in front of him. "You signed in your own hand. You named your price. Power. Obedience. Their worship. For your soul. Unless you need a reminder of what that looks like."

He's shaking now. Wet gasps. Fingers clawing at the wood like it'll save him.

"Mercy," he chokes.

"You don't get to speak her name." Selene's voice is steel behind me.

I press two fingers to his chest. Just above the heart. The skin blackens beneath my touch—veins spidering outward in jagged, pulsing webs.

"No," he whimpers. "Please, please—"

Cassian appears behind me—silent, towering, flame in his eyes. "Take what's owed, son."

I reach inside him—not for the flesh. But deeper down. I seize the thing he tried to sell and tried harder to deny.

His soul screams. It tries to run. I don't let it. He convulses. His back arches, a grotesque bowstring pulled too tight. Bones crack—one, then another, a sickening staccato of snapping joints and splintered cartilage.

Blood bubbles from his mouth in thick, frothing gurgles. From nose, eyes, ears. A flood of red, and then black—oily and unnatural.

The crowd watches paralyzed. Mouths open. Prayers dead on their tongues. Not a hymn left. Just the silence of people realizing God isn't coming. Not for them.

Obadiah's body jerks again. His spine snaps back, limbs flailing like a puppet whose strings are on fire.

He screams.

But it's not a sound a man should make. It's too deep. Too many voices layered at once. A howl of damnation, like Hell itself has come to collect its tithe.

Light erupts from his chest—black fire rimmed in red,

spitting shadows that twist and claw. The soul—his soul—rips free.

It fights. It thrashes, claws at the air, at me, at anything it can touch. But it's already mine. I close my fist around it. And drag.

It tears from his body like flesh from bone, screaming until the sound cuts off like a blade through wind.

Silence falls as his body slumps.

A husk—skin shriveled, eyes hollow, mouth locked open in a scream that never ends. Ash creeps from his pores. His robes sag. He collapses in on himself, no more than a ruin of bone and char.

I rise, breathing heavily.

Selene stares at me like she's seeing a god and a monster wrapped in one being. The pastor's blood is cooling on my fingertips. "No one touches what's mine."

The crowd stares. Then the chanting starts again. Not hymnals. Not prayers.

Screams. Stones.

The gallows may have fallen, but the reckoning has just begun.

Chapter Seven

SELENE

Obadiah lies crumpled in the dirt—what's left of him.

His skin has turned the color of old parchment, tight and cracked like earth in a drought. Charred around the edges. The lines of his face, once so full of arrogant smugness, are sunken in. As if something burned him from the inside out and left only the shell behind.

His mouth is open. Widened with a scream that never escaped. Eyes hollowed out and empty. Nothing in them.

His robes hang loose on his frame, barely clinging to the scorched remnants of flesh. Flakes of soot fall off his body with every breeze. He looks more like a statue than a man. Not made of marble—but of mud, waiting to be washed away by the rain.

A stiff gust of wind blows through the square, and part of his shoulder crumbles—bone and ash disintegrating into the air.

This is no death any of us have ever seen. Because this is judgement and not natural.

And I... I feel no remorse. Only that he deserved

worse. His end was an easy one compared to what his soul is about to go through.

In the crowd, I see Mercy and my father coming towards us.

They step toward the stage like ghosts themselves. Isaac's face is pale. His steps are slow. He looks uncertain. An expression I'm not used to seeing on Isaac Winscott. His hands tremble at his sides.

Mercy is right next to him. She won't meet my eyes. Her braid has come loose. Her face is blotched with tears and shame.

They stop at the foot of the platform. For a long moment, no one speaks.

Then Isaac lifts his chin and says, "What… what are you?"

His tone has no condemnation. Still a bit of defiance behind his shaky appearance.

I step forward. "I'm the one who was willing to do anything for her," I say, nodding toward Mercy. "The one you threw to the gallows so you could keep your precious pastor at the foot of the Almighty."

Mercy finally looks up.

"Selene," she breathes. But it's not the apology I was hoping for. She's just a wide eyed, broken girl who's finally seen the truth—and it's uglier than she ever imagined.

"I didn't know," Mercy whispers, hands trembling at her sides. "I was scared."

I stare at her—this girl I gave everything for. The one I was willing to end my life for. Give my soul for.

Mercy.

I thought seeing her whole again would bring peace.

But all I feel is emptiness when I look at her.

Because the truth I tried so hard to bury under duty and devotion is that it wasn't just for her.

It was never just for her.

I wanted to be the one who saved her.

Not Obadiah. Not God.

Me.

I wanted her to look at me the way they looked at him. With reverence. With awe.

I told myself it was love. Maybe some of it was. But love—true love—doesn't come with chains.

She didn't ask me to trade my soul. She didn't ask me to summon fire or demons or damnation.

She didn't ask. I never let her.

Because if I did… she might've said no.

Then I would've been just the sick girl's sister. Just another girl in Salem. Another name they could laugh at.

"I say I did it for you," I whisper, eyes still locked on hers. "But I actually did it for me." My fists tighten. My throat burns. "And for that, I'm sorry that I ever tried to save you."

She is alive. But I am free. Mercy flinches. Isaac doesn't even blink. He just stands there, mouth tight, arms crossed, like a father watching a daughter he never wanted finally get what she deserves.

The man steps beside me—closer now, a shadow in my periphery, heavy with heat and something I can't put my finger on. "She's not yours anymore." My head snaps to him. He isn't done. "She's ours. Duvain by bond. And blood, if it comes to it."

Isaac stiffens. Mercy's lips part, but no sound comes out.

Cassian steps forward towards me.

"This is Serenya," he says, gaze unwavering. "My bond. My equal. My soulmate."

Isaac stiffens. Mercy's lips part—shocked, maybe. A little squeak comes out.

Cassian doesn't give them any notice.

"These are our sons," he continues, turning slightly—one hand gesturing to the man behind him and the man beside me. "Evander. And Theron."

I feel the pulse in my chest before he says the words.

"You are bonded to Theron. As fate intended. As the realms have already begun to answer."

Theron looks down at me. I see love shining in his eyes. But that isn't possible. We have just met.

"Say your goodbyes."

Cassian. Serenya. Evander. Theron. My family. The only ones who seem to care about me.

I look at the Winscotts, face calm, voice calm—but something in me is breaking loose. "I don't forgive you." They go still. Mercy's lip quivers. Isaac's jaw tightens. "I don't owe you forgiveness. I don't owe you anything."

I turn from them and walk to the crowd. The broken townspeople who once called me a witch with froth on their lips. They flinch as I approach, like I might burn them with a look. Good. Let them feel fear for once. Real fear that they inflicted on all those other women.

"You think yourselves righteous?" My voice slices the square in half.

I face them all. Every last craven. Every bystander who watched. Every man who spit at my feet. Every woman who turned her face when I screamed. Every child clutching a cross as if it could cleanse the violence from their lineage.

"You think of yourselves as holy. Faithful. Just. But all I

see are cowards in cloaks. Sheep wearing the wool of wolves and pretending not to know what blood feels like."

Gasps ripple through the crowd. A few cross themselves. Others clutch their children tighter, like my words will infect them with the truth.

Good.

Let them be afraid. Let their hearts beat like mine did when they dragged me through the square—barefoot, bruised, bound.

"You let him preach judgment with fire on his tongue and hatred in his heart. You called it a sermon. You called it justice. You let your daughters hang while he wore their screams as scripture."

My voice begins to tremble. I feel Theron place his hand on the small of my back. He is giving me my power back. Not take over. Empowering me to take my vengeance.

"You watched me suffer. You watched me beg. None of you even flinched when Obadiah Crowe took over Salem. Not once. Instead, you wanted someone to hate more than you wanted someone to explain what you didn't understand."

I walk forward. My blood still paints my hands. My hair clings to my neck, damp with sweat and a rope burn from death that didn't quite stick.

"You called me a witch. You called me devil. You called me a lesson for the other girls to learn from. But hear me now! I am not your warning. I am your consequence."

The wind moves. The ash from Obadiah's remains stirs at my feet.

"You let him twist the name of the Almighty until it sounded like his own." I point toward the charred heap that used to be a man. "You called him a God amongst men."

Murmurs rise. The people are uncomfortable. Probably with the truth they never had to hear before.

"It wasn't just me. It was every woman who spoke too loud. Every girl who bled too soon. Every soul who questioned why your God only ever looked like Obadiah Crowe."

"You let your fear build the gallows. You did not fail because you believed in the wrong man. You failed because your faith cost us our lives and you still said Amen anyway." The square is dead quiet. "I will not carry your shame for you. I will not shut my mouth so that your vision of heaven remains clean. I was never the witch. You were."

My voice rises with the weight of every girl they silenced. "You worshipped fear and called it God. You listened to the so called devil and called it doctrine. And when he asked for a lamb, you handed him your daughters."

Gasps turn to sobs. But none come close. No one dares speak.

I take a final breath. "I will leave this town behind. But you will not leave what you've done. It will stain you. Forever. Because you will remember this day not as the day your witch fell into the flame—"

I turn back to the stage. To the ashes. To my new family.

"—but the day your lies did."

A hush falls over the square.

I grab Theron's hand and leave the rest behind. Because I do not belong to Salem anymore. I don't think I ever truly did.

They stare. Not like people—like ghosts who've just realized they're dead. All of them. Faces I once knew. Prayers still on their lips. Blood still on their hands.

Their town stands proud behind them—whitewashed walls, wooden crosses, smoke curling from hearths that never once warmed a single soul.

I close my eyes. I don't need a spell. Don't need a demon.

I am the reckoning. My fingers curl into fists and I feel the heat rise beneath my ribs. It climbs my throat like a scream too big for sound.

I open my eyes, and the wind halts mid breath. "Let judgment find you," I whisper, "as it found me."

The first flame blooms beneath my bare feet. The hottest a fire can be. White licks across, taking the gallows along with it.

I walk forward and point my body towards the church. The same one where they praised him. Where they condemned me. Let it rot.

"Witch!" someone cries.

"Monster!"

Let them name me. "Let your God save you now," I say to no one and to all of them.

They run. The ones who chanted. The ones who wept. Even the ones who stayed silent.

I turn once—just once—to look at what's left.

Smoke devours the sky. The flames sing louder than any hymn. And Salem… well Salem is burning.

Let them say it was the devil. Let them lie, like they always have.

But deep down… they will know.

They are the ones that built the pyre.

I only lit the match.

Chapter Eight

SELENE

I thought Hell would be fire and brimstone. I was wrong. The fire is there. But the heat never finds me. The realm we step into is nothing like the stories Obadiah told when we were children to scare us.

I breathe in the air around me. It tastes like storms and burnt metal. The mountain drops away beneath my feet, much higher and steeper than the rolling Appalachian mountains I'm used to.

The house is carved into the cliffside in the mountainous region of Hell. A shadow hewn from stone is perched above a river that isn't water at all.

It churns far below. Black molten fire waves out. The stars here don't blink. They watch.

"This is my home." Theron stops at the edge, hands in his pockets. "We can go to the beach later."

I blink at him. "That's not a beach. That's... hellfire."

He chuckles softly. "Technically, it's a river." I arch a brow.

"Old one," he adds. "Before borders and names. It runs

under half the realm. Some say it remembers the first war. Others say it started it."

I glance down at the molten tide, endless and slow. "And this is where you built your house?"

"Didn't want neighbors." He starts walking toward the arch at the end of the room. "Also," he says over his shoulder, voice jesting now, "the sound calms me."

He nods toward a corridor. "Come."

We pass a library first. It sits beneath a tangle of glowing roots that twist down like glass trees frozen mid-fall. Shelves stretch to the ceiling, curving into the stone itself. Every book hums softly, magic resting on the spines like dust.

I feel… wanted.

Theron doesn't look at me, but something about the way he slows—just slightly—as if he's waiting to see if I'll step inside, makes my chest tighten.

Wanted. For no other reason than the fact that I'm… me.

It's terrifying.

"That look," he says, finally glancing over his shoulder. "What is it?"

I hesitate. "You make it hard to believe that love doesn't exist."

His mouth curves. He's about to say something witty.

"Then I guess I've got work to do," he says, smirking. "Starting with making sure you never forget how it feels."

He walks back toward me like he knows exactly what he's doing. Maybe even worse—like he knows exactly what I'm feeling.

There's only a breath between us now. One shift, one heartbeat, and we'd touch.

My body stills. My pulse does not. It rushes in my ears similar to the river below us.

I've faced false prophets pretending to be kings. I've stood before death. But I've never felt this. Not the ache. Not the heat blooming under my skin. Not this overwhelming need to be *close* to another person. I didn't know I could want someone like this. It terrifies me down to my very core how much I want *him*.

"But you should know something." He lowers his head to the shell of my ear. "You'll never go unwanted again."

The words already settle like a promise in my bones.

I push him back, arms wrapping around his neck. I want to look into his eyes. To tell me the truth I need to hear before I feel anything more for him. This is not a jest to me. It can't be to him either.

"What is this?" I whisper. "What are we to one another?"

"Bonded," he says.

Bonded. That word settles heavy in my chest. Not a public vow in front of a minister. Or legal documents.

"It's not a vow," he says again, quieter now. "Not like mortals make, with promises they break or forget. This is something fate carves itself. Not everyone gets one."

I study him, trying to anchor my thoughts, but something inside me has already shifted—subtle, ancient, like a thread pulling taut.

"You're saying… fate chose us?"

He nods slow. "Yes. It did."

I swallow. "Then it's not a choice."

"It is," he says. "But not *who*. Just *how*."

My brow furrows.

"Fate draws the lines," Theron explains, voice low. "But we decide how to follow them. What to make of them. Whether to run, or stay, or grow into the space between."

He steps closer.

"But I believe in it," he adds. "I believe in us. I believe that we were meant to be."

He pulls me into his arms.

"You feel it, don't you?" he asks. "That pull? The way your magic doesn't bristle near mine. The way your soul doesn't want to run from mine."

I do. I feel it like heat under my skin. Like standing on the edge of something I thought I would be afraid of. But there is comfort in it. As if it was meant for me to harness.

"Then it's already happening," he murmurs. "You don't have to accept it at this moment, Selene. But it's there. It won't unchoose you."

He watches me as if he can feel the questions breaking loose behind my eyes. "But I want you to accept it," he says. "Not just the bond. *Us.*"

His voice doesn't tremble. He's not unsure. "The pain. The past. The pull. All of it."

I open my mouth… but there's nothing I have to say.

"I know we can grow into this," he continues. "Grow into each other. It doesn't have to be all at once. But fate doesn't make mistakes, Selene."

He pauses. Then takes a step back and turns away from me, before turning back. His eyes are blazing the color of Oxblood. I can see his soul peering through them. "I don't think it gave me you just to lose you."

I'm silent. The sound of the wind and the river crash against the windows. The air is supercharged with

"I accept you," I say. My voice doesn't shake. Even if I do… just a little. "Not just the bond. Not just the mark. You." His breath falters. It seems like he's been waiting lifetimes to hear those words from me. A thread or tether inside him just snapped in half. "I don't want something perfect," I whisper. "I want something real. Something we build with our own hands. Our own mistakes. Our own grace."

His eyes burn. He's dropped any walls he put up. He'll never need them again. Not with me.

"I want to grow into this," I say. "Into you. Into us. I want to learn how to love you—not because fate demands it, but because I can't *not*."

I reach for him. My hand over his heart. His over mine.

"Let us become," I breathe. "Let us be the ones who rise from all of the pain the mortal world has bestowed on us. I'm ready to love. I've been broken, but I'm ready to be healed."

He closes his eyes like the words hit him hard. Knocked him off his feet. His smile lights up my world and prepares me for an eternity of passion.

"Selene," he murmurs, "I would walk through every war, every curse, every version of time just to find you again."

He leans in. His forehead rests against mine.

We are not marked. We are *chosen*. I am not afraid of being loved.

I knew I felt something. Adrenaline completely changed my body chemistry. Something like a brand should hurt. Yet I don't remember that being so.

I look down at my hands. The same ones that clawed the gallows platform. That begged. That bled. That held the locket when I bartered with a demon to save a girl who wouldn't even look me in the eye.

"I have no home," I whisper. "No family. Not really. But you..." My throat tightens. " A love that transcends space and time. One where my soul sings to my other half."

"My soul has always been yours," he says, his voice rough with choked up emotion. "Fate just knew it before I did."

His lips brush mine, before diving back in for me. I can feel him memorizing the shape of my lips. This is going to change us forever.

When we finally break apart, the world has recalibrated around this moment.

I start to speak. Nothing comes to mind. I could be honest—or I could be foolish. It doesn't matter because he beats me to it.

His arms slip around my waist and he lifts me. One arm under my knees, the other around my back. Effortless. Like I don't weigh a single pound.

We reach the last door. He opens it with a touch. It's vast—not in a showy way, but like something carved from the hardest substance in the natural world. Maybe it isn't even... natural. The largest room I have seen in my lifetime.

A bed sits at the center, enormous and low to the ground, framed in carved obsidian that catches the silver light. The sheets ripple like liquid silk, black with hints of deep garnet when the moonlight touches them. To the right, a wall of glass stretches floor to ceiling, seamless—a view that steals the breath from my lungs.

The cliff drops straight down into the lake below, the water churning silver black in the dark. Above it, a balcony juts out. It's surrounded by jagged stone railings that curl like wings at the corners. No railings to stop you. Only air and wind and sky.

The moon here is wrong.

It hangs massive above the water, veined like stone and low enough to touch. It bathes the room in cold light, illuminating the bare stone floors, the rich velvet rug underfoot, the shelves tucked into corners with relics and books and weapons I can't name.

The fireplace isn't made of brick, but some kind of ancient bone and onyx, lit from within by blue flame.

He puts me down on the warm floor. I stand still in the center of it all. The stone floor beneath my feet, the silver moonlight painting my skin.

Behind me, I feel him. Theron.

Watching.

Waiting.

I turn slowly, my voice barely louder than breath. "What is the mark, really? What does it mean?"

"You bear my mark," he says, voice low. "Because your soul called to mine. It's not branding. It's not binding. It's a beacon. A claiming of what already was."

He steps close enough that the heat of him curls into my skin. I should bristle at that. But I don't.

"Then… what is a claiming?" I ask.

"It's not what it sounds like." A faint smile touches his lips. "It is not a conquest. It's a covenant."

I swallow.

His fingers graze my cheek. "To claim is to join completely. Soul, body, magic. There are no vows more sacred among my kind. No power is more dangerous—or more permanent."

I want that. To be claimed permanently. To show someone I belong to them. Heart and soul. "Show me."

His mouth finds mine.

Outside the bedroom window, lightning forks through the sulfur lit mist. I feel the power of the claim begin in the mark on my collar. My breath quickens. The air in here turns denser, richer, like molten honey laced with embers. I feel his lips in the hollow of my neck and a pulse between my thighs.

The marks glow faintly, in rhythm with my own heart-beat, and I realize with a start that the bond is not dormant. It is awake, aware, hungry. It thrums in me. I've chosen this. Him. There is no hiding from what I am.

He kisses me.

A raw sound escapes him. His hands slip to my waist. He moves lower until his hands are on my thighs.

I blink and feel a chill running through my body. I am bare in his arms. I don't feel ashamed. I am safe with Theron.

He is so much larger than I am. That doesn't matter to him.

Each kiss leaves a heat that travels inward, threading through muscle and bone until I am molten, a vessel for nothing but want. His hands slide down my ribs, thumbs grazing the softness beneath my breasts. He lingers there, reverent, almost worshipful, and then moves lower. I arch against him, desperate to feel more. He teases, he with-holds, and I realize with something like outrage that he is smiling against my skin.

"Are you laughing at me?" I demand, breathless.

He shakes his head, the ghost of a smile lingering. "I am marveling," he says. "At you. At this. Do you know how long I have waited for my soulmate?"

I cannot answer. His hand is between my legs now, cupping me, thumb finding the place that makes my vision white out. He is gentle, unbearably so, and it makes me want to scream. Instead, I grab his wrist and guide him harder, shameless, past caring about any of it. I want all of it—his hands, his mouth, the way the world blurs at the edges when the bond pulses with our shared need.

He kneels before me, a demon at prayer, and I want to laugh at the blasphemy of it but I can only gasp as he slides his tongue over my skin. He tastes me—there, yes, and everywhere—and the sensation is a holy wound, open and bleeding. The runes on his skin flare as I writhe and shudder, echoing the bloom of power in my own veins.

My virtue is still intact. I've never consummated a relationship. In my lifetime, I never thought I would.

Though, this is not how we were taught it would be in Sunday school. No pleasure for the woman. Only for the man to take what he needs with the female left to be impregnated.

When I surrender, I feel the bond shattering and healing and tightening all at once. The world splits in two, then rushes back together in a tide of electric blue and gold.

He lifts me again, easily, as if I weigh nothing, and carries me to the bed carved from midnight stone. The sheets are black as the sky outside, cool against my fevered skin. He looms over me, all shadow and lust and mercy, and for the first time I am not afraid of what people think. I want to be broken open, rebuilt with his hands.

He settles between my thighs, his cock heavy and dark, the head slick and glistening. For a moment he just watches me, his eyes so bright I have to look away. He guides himself to my entrance, nudging gently, waiting for permission I've never given to another man before. The bond glows at my collar and his arm. He puts his mark over mine as he thrusts deeper. I feel something snap. My virtue is disappearing from existence.

It hurts—oh, it hurts, but the pain is a burning sweetness, a prophecy fulfilled. He enters me again and again. Slowly, inch by inch, his jaw clenched, his body shaking with the effort of restraint. The breach is shocking, exquisite, and I cannot help but cry out, nails digging into his shoulders.

He stills, trembling, forehead pressed to mine. 6"Breathe," he whispers. "You're perfect. I have you."

I do as he says. The pain dissolves, replaced by fullness, heat, an impossible intimacy. He moves, shallow at first, then deeper, and the friction sets the bond on fire. The marks on our bodies sear, light leaking through skin, through bone, through the very fabric of this world. I can see the ocean outside the window, storm swept and infinite, the same storm inside me now.

Theron kisses the tears from my cheeks, tongue flicking over salt and skin. "You're mine," he says, voice thick with awe. "No one else. Never."

"Yes," I say, and mean it with a violence that astonishes me.

He ruts me with an unholy tenderness, every thrust a question, every answer written in the arc of my spine, the tremble of my limbs. I cling to him, legs wrapped around his waist, pulling him deeper, harder. The sheets twist beneath us. The storm grows, as if what we are doing pulls the storms from the heavens. When I break again, it is not alone. He goes with me, his roar muffled by my mouth, his hands locked in my hair, our bodies fused by something older than time.

After, he cradles me to his chest, the rhythm of his heart almost human. The bond settles, a new organ in my body, pulsing with quiet power. I trace the marks on his arms, each one a story, a sin, a secret.

"Are you all right?" he murmurs.

I nod. "Better than."

He laughs, the sound rough but so tender it makes my throat ache.

Outside, the sea is still aflame with lightning. Inside, the darkness is full of silver and gold, and I am remade, holy in his arms.

Chapter Nine

THERON

I wake to the sound of Selene breathing. Her head rests against my chest, her cheek tucked just over my heart. I don't remember pulling her close in sleep—but I must have.

My arm is wrapped around her, palm spread over the curve of her ribs like I'm anchoring her to me. My other hand rests on her hip.

I move her hair aside, exposing the mark etched into her skin—the Duvain seal, still warm with the connection from the claim.

My fingers drag slowly across it.

She rolls over to lay on her stomach, draping one leg over my thigh. Her spine is bare and long and too goddamn perfect for a world like this.

I tuck my other arm under my neck and pull her closer.

Her hair spills over her shoulders, tangled and damp at the ends, falling across my chest like ink in water. It smells like cedar. What I've come to think of as her personal

I trace the length of her back with my eyes first, then my fingertips.

I can count each vertebrae.

Not just because she's delicate, but because she's starved. Her skin clings too closely to bone, her waist fragile as if built from glass. The hollows at her ribs tell me that she was suffering. She hasn't eaten properly in a long time.

There are other signs. Rope burns circling her wrists like cuffs, a pressure bruise beneath her collarbone, skin rubbed raw where cloth must've chafed over and over, with no one to tend it.

She never tried to hide them or cover herself from embarrassment. She embraced the fact that they are there.

But see, that won't do.

I raise my hand over it. With a flick of my wrist, each one fades before disappearing.

Nothing shall harm my dear Selene ever again. She will never need a reminder of what her mortal life looked like.

She is undone… and unafraid.

If I could, I would bottle this version of her. Loose limbs, hair spilling everywhere around her, and love in her heart.

I can't wait to begin our eternity together. Because this —this—is the holiest thing I've ever seen.

She shifts in her sleep. Just barely—a quick stretch of movement that sends her hair brushing over my chest and her thigh sliding higher up my hip. Her breath catches like she's surfacing from the deepest sleep she's ever endured.

Her lashes flutter. A crease forms between her brows.

I brush a strand of hair from her face, fingertips as gentle as can be.

Her eyes blink open. For a moment, she doesn't speak.

She just looks in my eyes. Even though it's only been a short time since we met, she never has a mask on with me. What you see is what you get.

But this version of her, only I get to see.

"I didn't dream it?" she whispers.

"No," I say, voice low. "You lived it. We both did."

She exhales, slow. One hand slides across my chest, settling over my heart like it belongs there.

She leans in to kiss me again when the floorboard creaks. The door opens with a soft sigh.

"Theron." Evander's voice. This isn't like him. He knows that Selene and I would like to be left alone. That's probably why he didn't portal straight into the bedroom, even though the privacy he's affording us was the bare minimum of a slight warning.

I shift, rising onto one elbow. She stirs beside me, sheet slipping as she sits, holding it close around her. I straighten, spine falling into readiness, muscles remembering old instincts.

Evander stands in the doorway, torchlight casting his face in flame and shadow. His eyes flick to her, then back to me. He clears his throat.

"Sorry," he mutters. "Didn't mean to interrupt. But there's a problem."

I swing my legs over the edge of the bed, keeping the sheet covering me. "What kind?"

He steps fully into the room. "Tribunal issue. Something's wrong. You'll want to see it yourself. Both of you."

I nod once. "Give us a minute."

He disappears down the hall, leaving us to get ready.

I don't go to the armoire. It's just for show anyway. I close my eyes and think about what I want to wear and what Selene would be comfortable in. Cloth folds over me like memory. A long sleeved tunic, black with silver threading, settles against my skin like it was waiting. Across from me, Selene blinks.

She's wrapped in a velvet tunic, silver-black and soft as smoke, fitted at the waist and hemmed in rune stitch. Dark trousers follow, tailored perfectly to her shape, as if they'd always belonged to her.

"Woah," she says, blinking. "Okay. I want to learn to do *that*."

I chuckle, rolling my sleeves up to the elbow. "I'll teach you later," I say, smirking. "When your mind's not still halfway between here and wherever I just took you."

She pulls at the collar, and sniffs. "I smell clean."

"That's because you are," I say, already bracing for it.

Her eyes narrow. "I didn't even see a bath."

"That's because you didn't need one."

She gives me a look—half amusement, half suspicion. All Selene. "You're enjoying this too much."

"I earned it," I reply, unrepentant. I did. Every damn second of it. She belongs in this world—and to me—yeah. I could get used to this.

When I'm finished putting final touches, I turn to her, holding out my hand. She takes a deep breath has her fingers interlace with mine. Something is wrong. We just don't know how wrong—yet.

The chamber opens before us—vast, solemn, carved from obsidian and lava. I keep my grip on Selene tight. More for me than for her. She's quickly becoming my rock. My everything.

I've stood in this room a hundred times. Heard my father's voice carry from its center. Watched him rule without cruelty, but with certainty and conviction.

But today is different. Something feels evil among us.

We move forward. At the center, Cassian stands. Wings furled like dark blades across his back. He doesn't raise his voice. Doesn't posture.

I have never seen the wings of a demon. In fact, none of us but him have them. The tribunal willed them for the three. To show power amongst demons. No others shall have them.

My mother stands beside him, starlight braided through her hair like strands of power and mourning. Her chin is lifted. Her shoulders are sharp as a drawn sword.

The chamber holds no council. No semi circle of wisdom. No thrones of balance. Just a tribunal with my father at the center.

Tarrin enters first, draped in silver like a king who never earned his crown. His eyes sweep the chamber—cold and cruel. Calculating.

Erisen is right behind him, every inch a brute disguised as a believer in Hell's sacred tribunal. Crimson robes, rusted gold, armor etched with wards so old they stink of grave dirt.

I feel Selene tense beside me. The bond between us hums—tight and restrained. She knows these types of people. With what she has seen and been through. People aren't all that different.

Even when they bowed before the throne—even when they pledged loyalty to my father—my instincts prickled. Men like Tarrin and Erisen don't serve, they bide their time.

My mother said to trust my instincts. My father always said to trust the Tribunal. That's one of the few things they've never agreed on.

The feeling in my gut wasn't fear. It was a prophecy trying to speak before the rest of me was ready to listen.

"Let it be said," my father begins, voice calm but heavy, "that we tried. That peace was offered."

"Let the record show," Tarrin says, voice like ice, "that it was you who allowed your bloodline to disintegrate—*you* who struck a bargain and let your son mate with the same mortal that the deal was made with."

Erisen slams his palm on the table. "Not to mention she is considered a witch in the mortal realm. They only do that to evil."

Before I can react, my mother does. "That witch," she says, voice cutting, "saved a life. Something you clearly have no use for."

Erisen and Tarrin move to confront her. Evander pulls her behind him.

"Enough." Cassian's voice snaps across the chamber like a lash. "We do not punish love. Not in this house."

Tarrin turns to Cassian. The rage in his eyes says it all—he came to overthrow them. "Then it is no longer your house."

The world narrows. My breath stops—caught, suspended, a heartbeat dangling over a blade.

Serenya's fingers twitch at her side.

My hand reaches back instinctively, seeking Selene. Needing to feel that she's still here.

My father's jaw locks. But then the unthinkable happens. The floor splits.

Erisen murmurs a prayer I've never heard—each syllable a twisting, rotting sound that turns the room inside out on itself.

Sereyna creates a portal and grabs Selene, throwing her in it.

A rune circle flares beneath him, sickly purple light bleeding outward. Cassian's head snaps toward him. "Don't," he warns angrily. "Don't you dare—"

But Erisen just smiles. "We dare."

The explosion makes an ear shattering sound. Evander and I cover our ears while we rush to our father's side.

The ceiling groans. Obsidian walls crack like eggshells. The whole realm flinches, magic buckling under the force.

Cassian steps forward, arm sweeping out, enclosing all of us in one impossible gesture. "Behind me." A command. A shield. A father's final instinct.

Serenya reaches for him, but her magic flickers—weak, sputtering like a candle drowning in wind.

Tarrin's voice slices through the chaos. "Strip him."

Ancient magic lashes across Cassian's body—stealing power in glowing, tearing threads. His knees hit stone once—but he rises again, trembling, teeth bared, unbroken.

The ground ruptures open into a spiraling void.

Cassian braces his arms against the edges of the rift, holding it open with raw, impossible strength.

"GO!" he roars. "SERENYA—TAKE THEM—"

She tries. Gods, she tries. Blue fire pours from her hands, pushing back the pull of the void. Her hair whips in the gale. Her silver eyes lock on his.

"Cassian—" she chokes. "Hold on—"

"I am!" His voice cracks. "But they're—"

The spear appears before I even see Tarrin move. It's black as pitch and carved from something older than Hell itself. As he steps forward, I can see the look of understanding that crosses my father's face.

He knows what's about to happen. And still—still—he

shoves us back with a single pulse of power that flays the skin from my palms.

"NO!" Serenya screams.

But it's too late. The spear sinks into his chest. Cassian's face jolts—shock, pain, apology—before it stills. His hand reaches for her, fingers slick with his own blood.

Serenya's scream tears the air—but the portal swallows it. It swallows him. The rift snaps shut with a crack like a neck breaking.

Serenya steps forward, hand outstretched toward the empty air where her soulmate no longer exists.

"Cassian…?" Her knees hit the stone. "No," she breathes. "No, no—Cassian—my love—come back—"

Her hands shake. And then—they start to dissolve. White dust drifts from her fingertips.

"Mother—" I gasp, stumbling toward her.

Evander drops beside her, voice raw. "Stay with us—please—stay—"

But she's already fracturing. Her skin cracks like porcelain kissed by cold—light spilling through the seams.

"My soul…" she whispers. "Bound to his…"

Another crack streaks from her collarbone to her cheek. She lifts her eyes to us—her sons. And the pain there—it could birth a war. "My boys…" Her voice is fading. "Forgive them. But never forget what transpired here today."

I cup her face, shaking, burning from the inside out. "Don't go. Don't—Mother—don't leave us—"

She smiles. "You were my greatest light."

Evander bows his head into her shoulder, weeping in a way I have never—will never—forget.

She touches his cheek, her hand crumbling at the edges. "And you… you must be your brother's shield. He will forget his own heart. You must not."

Then—she looks at me, through me. Her silver eyes soften—knowing and certain.

"Protect her," she tells me. "The girl who called for revenge and love. You were made for her." Her lips tremble. "Tell your father…" A crack splits her ribs. "...I am coming."

Her final breath escapes in a soft, white cloud.

Then Serenya Duvain collapses into ash.

A roar tears out of me—raw, animal, world ending. Evander's sob cleaves the air beside it.

I fall to my knees, staring at the small, silent pile of white dust where a mother stood. A queen. A soulmate. A light.

Gone.

We don't wait for permission. We don't summon guards or call the Tribunal. They do not exist anymore.

We find them. The cowards didn't go far. Tarrin and Erisen are tucked away in the ruined west wing—where the wards have already begun to die, where magic frays like nerve endings too long exposed.

They're still arguing when we enter. By the time they notice we're here, it's too late for them.

Erisen tries to cast. But Evander stops him with a blade through the wrist. Tarrin steps back—but I'm already there, fire pooling in my palms and pure vengeance seeping through my bones.

"You broke her," I say. "You turned our father into a martyr for your evil cause. You tore this house in half."

Tarrin raises his chin. "We saved the realm—"

"No," I cut in. "You killed it."

I make to attack, to kill them. But their screams fill the air before I can so much as move. Briefly, I turn my head and see Selene there. Fire in her eyes. Blue flames seeping from her arms as the two men who ended my parents burn to the pits of Hell.

By the time she is done, there is nothing but ash and smoke. She tortured them like they did to the people I love.

My soulmate just proved how powerful she really is.

I look down at them, those two false kings.

"For Cassian and Serenya Duvain," Selene declares.

When we leave, we don't look back, don't give them anymore thought. They were left in the dark, alone, and forgotten.

Right where they belong.

Chapter Ten

SELENE

Time stops keeping itself.

Time slips past me—days, weeks, maybe longer. I can't keep track. Guilt festers in my chest. I killed Cassian. I killed Serenya. I'm responsible for it all.

The Council chamber burned for three nights. The fourth, it stopped pretending to be sacred. Its walls screamed. Its runes died. Its throne bled.

The Tribunal was destroyed. Now Hell runs a muck.

Demons began carving up the realm like meat. Territory changed hands in blood. The Wards fractured. The Veil Market sealed itself. The Ember Paths led nowhere. The Bone Garden refused to bloom.

I can't stay in this house anymore. Theron never blames me, but this whole thing is my fault.

He's standing in the ruins of the war room—where Cassian used to keep maps and blades and peace barely held together with threadbare hope.

He stares at nothing. His jaw locked. His hands are stained with magic and blood and guilt. And when he turns his head—just slightly, just enough to feel me watching—there's something in his eyes I don't know how to name.

I leave before he speaks, I have to.

I walk until the roads stop recognizing me. I walk until absence of sound becomes a companion louder than grief.

There is no place to escape to, so I build one in the places the realm forgot.

A cave deep beneath the molten rivers. An old root chamber in the bones of the world.

It was supposed to be a sanctuary. Now it feels like a tomb.

The pain hits before the memories do—sharp, splintering. Like my magic is turning inward, trying to tear itself free. It forces me to my knees, my fingers curling into the stone, trying desperately to hold myself together. But, I can't do it anymore, I break, no, I *shatter* into a thousand pieces.

Theron finds me fast. He doesn't speak—just pulls me into his arms, holding me tight enough to make me feel like I'm not ending, just for a moment.

"I couldn't save them," I whisper. "I should've done something—I should've stopped it—"

"Selene—"

"It was *our* mating that ended them, Theron. I'm the bad seed in all lives. Everything I touch turns to death. I made that deal with your father, started this chain of events." My voice faulters. "It's my fault."

Another set of footsteps fill the cave. Evander. I wonder if Theron told him what's happening.

"No," he says simply, stepping into the firelight. "It's not."

I try to shake my head, but the words won't stop.

"If I'd moved on—if I hadn't called upon a demon—your mother, your father—" My throat tightens. "They would still be alive."

Theron grips my hands, firm but gentle. "They made their choice," he says. "To save us. You didn't take that from them."

"You gave us a chance at finding a soulmate," Evander adds. "They gave their lives for that. We won't waste it by letting you drown in guilt that doesn't belong to you."

"I'm sorry I let you both down," I whisper.

"You didn't. So stop saying that," Evander says.

I shake my head, staring down at my hands. "You keep saying that, and still… part of me believes it."

"Then I'll keep saying this—until you believe me more." He glances over, one brow lifting. "Most people think I'm the dangerous one."

"You are." A flicker of a smile curves my mouth, and to my surprise, he laughs. Just once. Just enough to ease something in my chest.

"You know," he says, tipping his head back against the stone wall, "I always thought I'd have to protect my brother from someone like you."

I arch a brow. "Someone like who?"

His eyes slide to mine. "Someone who carries the weight of everyone else's choices on her shoulders. Who's lost too much and trusts too little. Someone who can stand by his side amidst all the turmoil eternity could throw at you both."

I exhale. "Now?"

He watches me for a moment longer. "Now I think you're the one who'd fight to protect him. Even from himself."

"So... does this mean we're officially family?" I ask, half teasing. Deciding it's best to just change the subject.

He groans dramatically. "Don't get mushy on me. I'll revoke it."

I laugh. Evander and I are going to get along just fine.

A sound like wind slips through my mind. *Come.*

I jump to my feet, heart pounding, eyes wide. "What the—did you hear that?" I say, scanning the cave like the stone might hold all of the answers.

Theron is already turning toward me, calm despite the panic thundering through my veins.

"We all heard it," he says. "You're not losing your mind."

"It spoke to me," I whisper. "Inside my head."

"It does that," Evander mutters, rising slowly. His voice is tight. Uneasy. "But that shouldn't be possible. The Chamber was destroyed."

My pulse won't slow. "What is calling us now?"

Theron's expression darkens. "Something is waking up."

I glance between them, then arch a brow.

"So you can conjure clothing, speak in thoughts, and now be summoned by ruined stone. Are there any other strange abilities you neglected to mention?"

Theron doesn't answer right away.

Evander lifts a hand. "He tried to summon soup once. Nearly burned down the eastern wing."

I blink. "Soup?"

Theron exhales through his nose. "It was a miscalculation."

"Clearly," I murmur, though the corner of my mouth twitches. "Remind me never to trust your culinary instincts."

Theron straightens. "It's calling," he says. "We need to go."

Evander gives me a look that is half resigned, half alert. "Best not to keep a haunted chamber waiting."

I nod once, pushing to my feet, the robe brushing my ankles.

"Lead the way," I say. "Before it decides to come find us. We don't need that happening."

Together we turn toward the path that will take us to whatever awaits.

The chamber is whole again. Thought, it shouldn't be. Just days ago the walls were scorched, the seal broken, and the throne cracked down the middle.

But now… now there are seven points arranged in a half circle above a glowing pentagram. The lines are seared into the ground itself—etched deep in radiant light, like the world cracked open to reveal something divine.

Six cloaked figures stand at their marks. The runes on their robes shine with a glow that is so blue, it is almost white.

The seventh point is empty.

The moment my eyes fall on it, something grabs hold of me. It's a pull that hits me in the spine sharply, like a hook behind my ribs. I gasp and stagger forward, feet moving without command. My breath shudders. My limbs feel distant.

"Selene—" That's Theron's voice, low and alarmed.

Evander says something too, but their words blur. The sound twists, muffled by the strange pressure building in my skull. It's like I'm under water and can't breathe. I can't turn back. I can't stop. I have no control. Because something wants me in that circle and my body obeys.

The moment I step into the circle, a brush of hot wind

rushes up from the glowing lines beneath my feet. It curls around my ankles, dry and electric, and I stagger back. This wind *knows* me somehow, it calls to something in my blood.

It begins. Shadowed fabric rises from the circle's edge. It climbs my body in large coils. Robes form around me. The folds ripple against my skin as they settle. A hood draws up over my head without touch. A veil shields my face from those around me. When I look down, I can barely see my hands.

The seventh figure has joined the circle.

Me.

I glance sideways. The six figures remain deathly still. Their cloaks ripple faintly in the heat, hoods low, faces lost in black holes except for the shining glow of pupils. They feel eternal and sacred. They are unapproachable.

A voice touches my mind, filtering through in a way that seems unreal. *Tap into the power.*

It is not a request. But a direction. I feel no fear or anger.

So, I do as it says, with a sharp inhale, I let the bond open.Magic stirs in me, uncoiling like smoke from an ember. It threads through my limbs, lights my senses.

Seconds after I open my eyes, I *see* them. The blurry look of women under their cloaks. Their faces aren't clear but I can feel them.

They all turn, as though they are one. Their gaze fixes on Theron, then Evander.

When they speak, it shakes the space beneath my feet. "We are the Council. The Tribunal is over. The Council has begun." There is something strange about the words. The voice is as one and indistinguishable from one another.

One of the voices—woven between the others—is

mine. I hear myself in them. Not as Selene. As something else. Part of the chorus. Part of the Council.

"You must leave," our voices say. "There will be a gathering. But not now."

Theron scowls. "She's not a prisoner."

"She is part of the flame," the Council replies. "And the forge is not yet done with her."

He steps forward. "No," he says flatly. "I'm not leaving her."

The seven of us do not move. My pulse hammers beneath my skin. My mind is full of unspoken questions.

One of the members lifts an arm, pointing the cloaked hand to the Duvain brothers.

"You will wait outside the chamber," the Council replies. "She will return when it is time."

Theron steps beside Evander, jaw locked. "If anything happens to her—"

"Nothing will harm the girl," they say.

"I'll be right outside," he murmurs. "You're not alone."

I nod. He can't see that, though. He is looking to where I walked to, but not at me. That's because a cloak dropped. I moved. I'm in the middle, not on the end. There isn't a way for him to know who I am.

They turn and leave. Once the door to the chamber closes and locks, the fire dies and glowing lights appear.

One by one, the figures lower their hoods.

I brace myself for judgment. Instead, I find recognition.

The first woman is tall, her dark braids woven with ash strands that catch faint firelight. Her flame scarred skin glows faintly as she meets my gaze.

"They burned me in France," she says simply. "Fourteenth century. For speaking to wind. For reading the stars.

I walked out of the flames, and the priest who watched became my tether. I am Maeryn."

Beside her, another woman's posture is elegant, unmoving. Ink black hair. Eyes like winter hail. "Kievan Rus. Tenth century," she says in a voice just above breath. "They taught me to obey. Taught me to never be insolent. I learned how to weaponize both. I am Sivara."

The third doesn't speak right away. She studies me, eyes knowing all. She is not from my time, but a century or more before. "Nyra," she says eventually. "Athens. Fifth century. They took my voice. I made them listen anyway."

Then I feel movement. Someone coming close to me. A golden skinned woman with lips the color of wine and the kind of smile that pulls people in and poisons them as a parting gift. "They thought my worth was in how I looked," she hums. "So I turned it into leverage. Sicilian court. Twelfth century. I'm Vireya."

A figure moves like fog. Her veil shimmers in the low light, and when she speaks, it's as if the walls bend to hear her. "England," she murmurs. "Thirteenth century. They called me mad because I heard what they couldn't. I didn't break. I just bent the clock. I am Serelisse."

I don't realize I've taken a step back—until the last one enters my space like a sunburst.

Hair wild. Skin sun-warmed. Eyes like cracked light. She's grinning, like she's *enjoying* this. "There are no records of me," she says cheerfully. "Because I burned them all. Numidia. Second century. My mate sees everyone's past—except mine. I like it that way. Elowyn."

They stand around me—not to close the circle, but to complete it.

Maeryn meets my eyes. "We came from different worlds. Different histories. But we all ended here. Bound by a soulmate. Loved unconditionally. Now we are asked to lead. For the time being."

Sivara's voice follows, soft but sure. "You complete the circle. Every one of us comes from a long line of women tortured and abused by men in our time. It is our duty to regain order."

Their eyes are on me—six lifetimes of defiance. They are just like me. Unashamed and strong. We changed the mortal world. Now it's time for us to change the immortal one.

It's my time now.

Like all of these women, I rise to the occasion.

Epilogue

SELENE

Owen is pacing along the length of our living room. "And you're just... still on the Council?"

I glance at him. He doesn't stop.

"They stripped all the Duvains of our names. Even Bella. And somehow *you're* still on the throne?"

I know why he feels betrayed. He thinks that I made the vote unanimous. But he has no idea the council runs on a majority. No matter what, my vote didn't count.

Arabella lifts her hand and grabs his shoulder. "Owen," she says. "You know that was my fault."

He turns to her. "Bella—"

She shakes her head. "I made the choice. I turned my back first. Don't blame her for what the Council had to fix."

"We didn't strip the name, Owen," I cut in softly. "We sealed it."

He scoffs. "Same difference."

"It isn't," I snap. "The name was always meant to be

one. Whole. Not split between bloodlines and vendettas and prophecy."

He flinches at that last word.

I step around the coffee table, stand in front of my nephew. "You and Bella were never supposed to fight against each other. You were meant to fight alongside each other."

He looks away.

"We had to keep fate in balance," I say. "And sometimes that means giving you a little push—so you can decide how to put it back together."

The doorbell rings.

Owen blinks. "Who the hell—"

I smile at them as the door opens.

Caelum walks in first—tall, broad shouldered, golden eyed. There's always something just slightly unreal about him, like the air forgets how to settle when he's near.

Thayer slips in behind him, quiet and lean, with that streak of silver in his dark hair that somehow makes him look both ancient and ageless. He nods to me, that familiar flicker of dry humor already in his gaze.

Serevin is all dark grace, moving like a shadow dressed in silk. He's the one who watches, who always knows more than he says. Matthias is a walking storm. Big, scarred, brutally handsome, with a grin like he just dared the world to hit harder.

They're demons, yes. Dangerous. Powerful. Each of them could level cities with a thought.

But mostly—they're family.

Not by blood, but by something stronger. Survival. Loyalty. Some twisted, cosmic affection that none of us ever bothered to name out loud.

Before I can speak, the chaos arrives.

Voices spill from the hallway, footsteps echoing against the stone floor. The rest of the Duvain family filters in from the back patio, still blinking from the glow of the fluorescent river outside—an otherworldly tide that only appears this time of year.

They were out watching it together, probably arguing about constellations and whose turn it was to bring in dessert.

Now they're here.

Julian appears like he's been waiting for the cue. "Uncles," he announces grandly, holding out his arms like a royal greeter. "Bless us with your questionable wisdom."

Owen elbows him. "Last time Serevin gave me advice, I ended up cursed *and* exiled."

"That's because you took *Matthias's* advice first," Lucas calls from the kitchen, already stealing a grape like this is a comedy rehearsal.

"I regret nothing," Matthias says.

"I regret *everything*," Caleb mutters, walking in with two wine glasses and no wine.

Adrian raises an eyebrow. "Is it too late to form a splinter faction and pretend we're the reasonable ones?"

"You're a necromancer," Damian says, casually tearing off a piece of bread. "Your entire aesthetic screams unreasonable decision making."

"Boys," I warn.

All seven freeze. For two full seconds.

Then Seth, without missing a beat continues the conversation. "Technically, we're all grown men."

Lucas hurls a roll at Owen, who ducks. It bounces off the wall and lands directly in Caelum's open hand.

He looks at it, then up at them. "Is this a ritual offering?" he asks flatly. "Or just an act of war?"

Julian grins. "Depends who you ask."

Caelum doesn't smile. He never really does. But something in his eyes gleams when he turns to me.

He walks past the table, ignoring the noise, the bickering, the plates being passed without purpose.

He doesn't stop until he's right next to me. "Are you ready?" he asks, voice low enough that only I can hear it.

I stop putting fruit on the tray and look at him. "For what?"

He looks around the room—at the laughter, the mess, the family we've built. Before returning his gaze to mine.

"For when all this breaks," he says quietly. "Because the world, Selene—" His fingers close around the roll. He crushes it in his palm. "—is about to fracture."

It finally hits me. Someone's coming for the Duvains. This time, we might not be enough to stop them.

Coming Soon in the Shadow Brides Series

Stellan and Talia found their happily ever after.

Now it's time for Opal Greer.

The girl no one wants.

The blacklisted one.

The ghost in designer heels.

But the only one who can handle her is Dante Valera.

The Society made a match. The paperwork's ready. All that's left is the signature.

Welcome to Underground Vegas.

Try not to lose your soul.

The Damaged Bride releasing January 15, 2026

Up Next in the Devil's Bargain Series

He's never been in a hurry for anything.

She's spent her whole life giving too much to everyone else.

But Sloth isn't about to wait.

He's about to take his time… because he refuses to destroy something beautiful.

Enemies will return. The world is about to fracture.
Coming March 2026

Want More?

Want more of Selene and Theron?

See how they defy tradition and seal their bond in a demon wedding that even fate didn't see coming.

Read their full wedding scene here: https://dl.bookfunnel.com/tor2ute6p0

About the Author

Sara McClaflin writes romance with feelings, flaws, and just the right amount of emotional damage. Her stories are character-driven, morally gray, and often ask one very important question: what if love was a little dangerous—and we liked it that way? After years of reading and reviewing books with too much angst, she finally started writing her own.

She lives on the West Coast with her husband, their chaotic dog, and more book boyfriends than she's willing to admit. Her TBR pile is a cry for help, her playlists are 80% heartbreak, and she's always chasing the next character who'll ruin her in the best way.

Newsletter Sign Up: https://subscribepage.io/saras-newsletter

amazon.com/stores/Sara-McClaflin/author/B0CR8VHBHJ?ref=sr_ntt_srch_lnk_1&qid=1761260490&sr=8-1&isDramIntegrated=true&shoppingPortalEnabled=true

instagram.com/authorsaramcclaflin?igsh=NTc4MTIwNjQ2YQ%3D%3D&utm_source=qr

facebook.com/profile.php?id=61551822185090&mibextid=wwXIfr&mibextid=wwXIfr

(54)Sara McClaflin | Romance Author (@sara.mcclaflin) | TikTok

goodreads.com/author/show/47632250.Sara_McClaflin

https://www.threads.com/@authorsaramcclaflin

Also By

The Devil's Bargain

Wicked Union– A prequel novella (Liora and Evander's story)

The Devil's Canvas

Gilded Lies

Unholy Vows (Selene and Theron's Story)

The Shadow Brides

Veil of Fire

Wildflowers & Whiskey (1.5)

The Huntington Brothers Series

Destined for Love

Tangled Hearts

Promises to Keep

Standalone Novels

The Keeper's Secret

Love on the Edge

Anthologies

Head in the Clouds: A Romantic Comedy Anthology

Desperate: A Deadly Thriller Anthology

Did you love *Unholy Vows*? If you enjoyed the story, I would be so grateful if you took a moment to leave a quick review. Thank you for reading, for your support, and for spending time with these characters. I can't wait for you to see what happens next!

www.ingramcontent.com/pod-product-compliance
Lightning Source LLC
LaVergne TN
LVHW090529110826
845146LV00003B/1032

* 9 7 9 8 9 9 9 1 7 7 8 1 0 *